W9-ACW-916

The Blind Owl

Sadegh Hedayat

The Blind Owl

TRANSLATED
BY

D. P. Costello

Grove Press
New York

Printed in the United States of America

ISBN-13: 978-0-8021-4428-7
eISBN: 978-0-8021-9642-2

Grove Press
an imprint of Grove/Atlantic, Inc.
154 West 14th Street
New York, NY 10011

Distributed by Publishers Group West

www.groveatlantic.com

The Blind Owl

INTRODUCTION

AMONG THE MANY PLACES I WAS FORBIDDEN TO GO AS a youth, was through the pages of a book that didn't even exist in our bookshelves. We had it all: walls and walls of the apartment I grew up in in suburban Los Angeles were lined with books, Persian and English. But there was one book, a notable book, we did not have a copy of, whose absence I was soon enough made to not just feel but to crave so ardently that it almost makes sense to me why I'd end up here, of all places.

I was barely double-digits when I first heard the title *Buf-i Kur. The Blind Owl*—it sounded not unlike the titles of my children's storybooks. When I inquired about it my father said it was a masterpiece of Persian literature, written before he was born. *What was it about?* I asked. Silence. *Is it about a blind owl?* Silence. *Do we have it?* I asked. There was something in my father's uncharacteristic reticence that made me push further. Every few years the book would inevitably come up in conversation and I would prod, but still nothing but that same silence.

My teenage years could be characterized by obsessions with all sorts of things I knew nothing about, and *The Blind Owl* was no exception. I was determined to get my hands on our copy. My father, with a particularly oily smile: *We have no copy.* I was shocked: *Why? What is the deal with this book? Have you read it?* My father: *Of course. Everyone in Iran has read it.* The logical complaint: *Then why can't I?* It was then that my father, suddenly desperately grave, told me that the reason we didn't have a copy—the reason, if he could help it, that I would never get my hands on one as well—was that, apparently, it had caused many suicides in Iran after it was published. Silence. *And, well, if you must know, the author also committed suicide.*

Back then I was already knee-deep in Woolf, Plath, Sexton, Hemingway, and, hell, Kurt Cobain had just ended his life—suicide had a behemothic allure to me. This made me want it all the more.

But I was not going to get it, not for a while. And then the moment I went to college and forgot all about it, suddenly one summer break when I was home, my father brought me a copy, an English translation. He seemed embarrassed. *Here. But don't read it.* Eyes downcast, fidgeting, silence. *Or maybe it's not as bad in English. I don't know.* More silence. *But don't think about it too much.*

It was finally mine. For a few days I rejoiced and just stared at it on my shelf, as if it were some magical object that was best observed but barely handled. And it sat there for years. Having possession of it finally made it less desirable; knowing at any moment I could go there made it less illicit.

That was my first phase. My second phase was the one in which I wanted to read it but just couldn't. It was no doubt the superstition about suicide. In my early twenties, I grew more and more depressive—suicide became less dazzling, more haunting—and the book felt like a loaded gun in an unlocked cabinet, as it sat there, gathering dust, unfiled, flat, virginal, in opposition to the other lovingly aged books on my bookshelf. I never took it with me to college, never took it anywhere. Periodically I would think about it and think about approaching it, but again, like something that had the power to kill or at least curse me, I stayed away. I was waiting for an era where my magical thinking would look as absurd as my father's did to me in my sunnier youth.

It took beginning my own novel to go there. The long form, it has always seemed to me, has the power to really shelter you, keep you covered and protected for several years, and so in that era, for the first time in my life, I experienced no fear. I didn't have confidence either, but at least I didn't have fear. I finally picked up the book, once in my parent's home again, and read it fast, all the way through in one sitting, as if the words were on fire, as if it would burn me if I lingered too long, the magical thinking not altogether dust just yet.

But that was only part of it. The other part was simply the content. It was the most disturbing thing I had read (and I had read many disturbing things by then; I was deeply attracted to them, in fact). But this made me feel sick for days. I thought about announcing anemically at dinner that after fifteen years of wondering, I finally knew. I had read it. But I couldn't bring it up. I never told anyone I had read it.

I started to feel spiritless, to put it euphemistically, once the novel was done. Several brushes with bad luck had collided to create a most calcified dolor, so potent that nothing scared me, not depression, not death, nothing. In searching for my novel's epigraph, my mind turned to, appropriately, *The Blind Owl*. I picked one: "*I thought to myself: if it's true that every person has a star in the sky, mine must be distant, dim, and absurd. Perhaps I never had a star.*" It was in many ways an epigraph that did not suit my novel, but it certainly suited *me* at the moment. The most dismal side of me could think of no other author, no other work, to jinx myself with.

And then the part of me that believed I would get over this wanted everyone to know about this breathtaking novel that had, over many personal peaks and valleys, grown to mean the world to me.

And here I am again, still wishing that on everyone who has yet to touch these pages. In reading it again and again over the years, I have become more and more immune to its horror and more and more ensorcelled by its masterfulness. It is, first of all, a novel that demands countless readings; it demands that you become a student of it. As I became a novelist in my own right, I grew less afraid of its powers and more attune to its mechanics, but I never stopped feeling wholly humbled by its profoundly radical aesthetics. And Sadegh Hedayat, who I learned more and more about, became one of my most cherished literary icons.

Which is why I was ecstatic and overwhelmed to introduce Western audiences to the new edition of D. P. Costello's 1957 translation. Of course, my first thought was that it seemed embarrassing that I'd even be a liaison in this mission—I could imagine Hedayat rolling his eyes at me through his thick black-framed spectacles and wisecracking something along those lines. I thought of the judgment of every Iranian I knew who, without a blink of an eye, would swear ultimate allegiance to *The Blind Owl*. It is that type of national treasure that elicits the most indeed-blind unconditional ardor. Even if they don't stand behind certain storyline special effects or are confounded by its many baffling twists and turns, they consider it very much *theirs*; Hedayat feels so much in our blood that it's hard to remember he came to be in Iran and not the other way around.

Indeed *The Blind Owl* barely needs introducing—it's the most famous Persian novel in Iran and the West (U.S. and Europe), and Hedayat is without argument the father of Persian modernist fiction. But *The Blind Owl*'s revolutionary surrealism is the exception to even Hedayat's own rules, as most of his stories are in the realist vein, often wryly comic in satiric works or resolutely nostalgic in nationalist-realist works. It is not an easy read and yet, against all odds, it is the most renowned literary work of twentieth-century Iran, unreadable to the masses, one would assume, with its opaque symbolism, corkscrewed coding, warped psychological landscape, and otherworldly thematics. But Hedayat's prose has always been accessible in its simple style, much like Edgar Allen Poe—his closest Western kin, along with Kafka, one can argue, both of whom he held in high regard—who is often taught in American middle school. Perhaps the very prose, coupled with its fabled notoriety, has made it an essential literary hand-me-down in Iran. I'd like to think the Iranian disposition is simply more all-embracing of the experimental in art, as well as more inviting of investigations into the darkest crevices of the human soul.

But for whatever reason, it is one of Hedayat's only forays into such horror. It is a masterpiece of what eminent Hedayat scholar Homa Katouzian calls "psycho-fiction"—that which "reflects the essentially subjective nature of the stories, which bring together the psychological, ontological, and metaphysical in an indivisible whole." In that way it feels like his most "real" work, even in its almost mystical fabulism. It feels as if it exists independently of its author, as if it were a relic, without tangible attribution, like a holy scripture, a certain unearthly authenticity reaffirmed by the rawness of its feverish confessional tone—and parallels to Hedayat's bio, of course. And that, of course, renders this frightening tale all the more frightening.

In the end, the book only reflects certain elements of Hedayat's life. There is the perpetual haze of opium which, based on whatever account you subscribe to, Hedayat was an occasional dabbler or a hopeless addict. And there is, of course, Hedayat's fascination with India—he studied Middle Persian in Bombay, where he apparently penned *The Blind Owl*—in the core myth of the narrative, the chilling "trial by cobra," which the half-Indian narrator's Hindu dancer mother, Bugam Dasi (the novel's only named character), initiates, igniting the whole nightmare premise of story. And there is Hedayat's vegetarianism, which he fully dedicated himself to in India, portrayed in the novel's herbivoric undertones by the narrator's consternation over the routine sight of a local butcher at work. And there is Hedayat's notoriously asexual or homosexual bachelorhood—again depending on which account you subscribe to—in the novel's sexual anxieties and impotency qualms with multiple images of stunted virility, from various stills of lascivious and yet unsatisfying elderly male lovers to ultimately the novel's climax, which, as brilliant Hedayat scholar Michael Beard points out, is an *actual* climax involving a knife taking over what the organic phallus fails to fulfill.

And, of course, there is the sense of an eternally alienated outsider's cast on the whole novel, a despair we know was definitely Hedayat's, which likely led to his suicide by gassing himself in 1951. He carried an inconsolable loneliness in walking through the world as well as in the artistic rendering of it. Hedayat's narrator is either representing his nightmare through painting or by confessing it through writing, but in either case he lets us know that the creative act is his way of dialoguing with his shadow. . . which Beard skillfully points out could very well be *us,* the audience beholding the narrator's, as well as Hedayat's, art.

Everything else, we could say, is a fiction, rooted in sources so entirely mysterious that indeed *The Blind Owl,* while feeling "real," seems to be born of a world all its own, a tale far beyond the experience of its author, any author—certainly, luckily.

Hedayat was thirty-three when the work was first self-published in India, its initial incarnation being fifty copies of handwritten text distributed for circulation among friends with a "not for sale in Iran" note on it, due to Hedayat's initial discouraging encounters with Iranian censors. Iran, two and a half decades after its Constitutional Revolution, and a decade after the tail-end of the Qajar dynasty and the beginning of the Pahlavi dynasty with the establishment of Reza Shah's reign, had experienced rapid authoritarian modernization and secularization with the British and the Russians salivating over the prospect of Iranian oil, while the Shah's regime created invisible shackles over the masses through propaganda and censorship. This was how Iran turned Western and fast, a place where Islamic traditionalism and Western modernization were at a tug-of-war. This era of cultural crossroads heralded many decades of such awkward seesawing of old and new, tradition and progress, crises of identity of which Iran still, clearly, is deeply embroiled. For Hedayat, neither the clergy nor the monarchy held the answers, neither the common man nor the elite intelligentsia; he was at once at odds with not just his country, as many have been quick to conclude, but his era. Sadly, one could assume he'd be no better off in this era, as he would, no doubt, like myself, be an immigrant in an exile of no foreseeable end.

After serialization in the journal *Iran* in 1941–1942, the history of *The Blind Owl* has been largely a hide and seek with authority. It was published again in 1993 but censored, banned from the 18th Tehran International Book Fair in 2005, and publication rights were withdrawn as a part of a 2006 sweeping purge. But it's a testament to the text that it has never come close to a circulation hiatus among the people.

Was it simply the gore that made it unacceptable to the establishment? I think it was its intertwining of cultural dualities, which was quintessentially more Hedayat than any other aspect of the work. Novelistic prose did not really exist in Persian before the twentieth century, and whereas the early Iranian novels were historical novels written by academics and intellectuals, this was something altogether different from even its different status as a novel. Hedayat was, after all, pretty much bicultural, and *The Blind Owl,* as many have declared, is in certain ways a Western novel following and even making indentations in the European tradition. Hedayat was in many ways partially French: he attended a French school, the St. Louis missionary school in Tehran; he had a state grant to study in France, and he himself claimed he was a lifelong student of French literature; he died in Paris and was buried in the famous Père Lachaise cemetery. He was as Western as he was Eastern and the same could be said for the novel—it's truly Middle Eastern or West Asian, one could say. And this is arguably the Iranian condition or at least its modern condition, that the left and right of Iran always feared to face—a nation of constant conquest, perpetual displacement, and exile, a country of homeland seekers with a destination only in their ancient past. Hedayat could not find solace in Tehran society and yet in Paris he could not find peace either. He was the Iranian nationalist who, fed up with the corruptions of church and state alike, was perpetually looking westward; he was also the foreigner in Europe, whose daily life was endless Visa applications and intense economic hardship, whose eyes were cast to the comforts of his mother country where he was of the aristocracy. And like these contradictions, so existed *The Blind Owl,* whose biggest challenge, one could assume, was that of audience—many Western literary references were lost on Iranian audiences and many Iranian folkloric descriptions were alien to Western readers, and yet the book held its place among both readerships. Influence spotting has led scholars all over the place, from the implausible to the certain, academics claiming Buddhist doctrine, Jung, Rilke, Poe, Sartre, and Kafka in its pages—but no matter what, no one denies the book is as Eastern and Western as it rejects both as well. One of the aspects of *The Blind Owl* that kept it alive for me while working on my own novel—a truly hyphenate work in that it is equally Iranian and American—was that it felt like our first truly hyphenate work, Hedayat embodying the *first* true Iranian immigrant, a both reluctant and ecstatic pioneer of the West.

Part of the agreement in setting on the journey of a truly hybridized work is accepting its polarities. With *The Blind Owl,* we are taught to read a novel all over again—in its pages there exists a collection of codes, variants, repetitions, cycles . . . and there is no index, glossary, footnoting, or critical-analysis consensus even. We are left alone, very alone, to read unlike we have ever read before.

We have on one hand a Gothic romance narrative and on the other hand an expressionist whodunit allegory, both equally problematized by the innovative structure: a novel in two novellas, its twin narrative sections playing for and against each other. In Part I, our narrator is a painter whose vocation is to paint a single picture on pen cases. In Part II, there is no mention of him being an artist and instead he is the confessor, a writer telling his story to, we can assume, save whatever is left of his sanity. Interestingly, the pen case holds the tools of a writer, while the first part exists as a distorted dream recollection of the second's summarized confession of the past. In other words, the first part is the present in the form of a dream, while the second is the past in the form of a confession—and already, the algorithm is a precarious one, no doubt.

But the dualities continue. The artist of the first part, Beard notes, is immersed in a platonic love state, given the task of representing his muse, the beautiful young woman who, like an angel, appears at his door only to die in his bed. She opens her eyes for a moment within the clasp of death, apparently so our artist can render them in his art, and then she is nothing but fodder for an exhausting burial that involves one of the novel's many old men, a sinister hearse driver. In Part II, everything is the first part's negative: the writer is feverish from carnal love for his cheating whore-like wife who is just a door over, holding court in her bedroom, which he, the husband, banishes himself from in favor of his tomb-like room. But what is ingenious about this simple set-up is all the multiples and recyclings and variations on not just a few finite themes but a few finite images. Beard notes the novel features the same actors playing different characters over and over. We have several old men: uncle, gravedigger, odds-and-ends man, the narrator; we have several young women as well: the woman on the pen case, the woman he spies outside the ventilation hole of his home, the angel at his door, the wife, the wife's brother, his mother. Scenes also mirror one another, just as action and art imitate each other; the scene on the pen case reflects the scene outside the ventilation hole, which mirrors the scene on an ancient jar unearthed at the girl's burial in the first part, which mirrors his mother's final dance. Not only is this style simply dazzling in its innovation, it points to an opposite effect—recycled communal imagery that implies a certain paucity of the imagination or miserly economy of action or, just simply, tiring reworkings of a scenario for it's own sake. Such rearranging, scrambling, and skewing of an already sleek novel's minimalist furnishings is just not done in fiction, then or now or ever, we can assume. It requires, at its very least, the closest of multiple readings and, at its very most, conscientious code-breaking dissection.

In referencing Michael Beard so many times, I think it's important to point out he wrote perhaps the greatest study of the novel, *Hedayat's* Blind Owl *as a Western Novel.* It inspired me to write to him and ask how he came about discovering this book. It was apparently while he was in Peace Corps training in Iran. "I had a fever the evening I read it. I had recently picked it up in the reading room and figured it might be a good companion. It was a perfect companion. Alone, late at night in an unfamiliar place I felt in tune with it. It was a seductive book even before I understood it. The memory of it lingered after we went to our sites (I was teaching high school in Rafsanjan, then a small town). In Peace Corps pedagogy you speak before you can read, and as I was slowly becoming literate in Persian, it was one of my textbooks. I began to read it slowly, with a dictionary at hand, and it became one more teacher." Beard went on to write that when working on his dissertation on it, many years later, he "became very interested in the elegant way Hedayat rethought European traditions."

What he concluded our exchange with interested me most, a sentiment absent from his seminal book: "Later I began to think about Hedayat in biographical terms. I have no doubt that melancholy ingrained in his character led to his suicide, but I also believe that there is an exuberance in his writing that counteracts it. The expression of melancholy is not the same thing as melancholy. It may hold melancholy at arm's length."

This, I think, is the key to appreciating the nightmare-scape of *The Blind Owl,* once you piece its puzzles, catch on to its games, and read by its rules. The prose contains an energy that reminds one that even though Hedayat was quite depressed for much of his life, he was also the man spotted holding court in various cafés in Paris and Tehran alike, always entertaining huge groups of friends and followers and everything in between. We can see in this book, as well as in all his writing, not what might be implicated in his untimely death, but what prevented it for so long. And this is why I believe no reader could, as the myth went, contemplate death at their own hands after reading it—*The Blind Owl* is not a triumph of story, it's a triumph of art. It doesn't tell you how to live or die, but it does teach you a few things about how to create. And what is more life-affirming than that?

Only years and years after my father forbade me to read it and eventually gave in, did I understand that all the fuss might have been a personal one as well. After all, I came to see myself as not a successor or descendent even, but as a child of Hedayat—and almost literally, as my father had more than a few similarities with Hedayat. He too was an adamant Middle Persian hobbyist and Zoroastrianism enthusiast who endlessly romanticized pre-Islamic Persia to the point where the walls of our living room were entirely plastered with color-copied clippings out of *Smithsonian* magazine, featuring Sasanian plates and Achaemenid relief images. Plus, it was his vegetarian tendencies that made a vegetarian out of me. He was not a writer, of course, but he made one out of me. Not to mention he raised a pensive, brooding, loner kid who never felt quite at home in her imagined there or her literal here. And so, of course, it had to be him who kept me from reading it for so long.

Given the usefulness of his tactics with respect to that, I'll then pass on what got me to these pages: refrain, reader, from reading this book, whatever you do.

You've been warned.

1

THERE ARE SORES WHICH SLOWLY ERODE THE MIND IN solitude like a kind of canker.

It is impossible to convey a just idea of the agony which this disease can inflict. In general, people are apt to relegate such inconceivable sufferings to the category of the incredible. Any mention of them in conversation or in writing is considered in the light of current beliefs, the individual's personal beliefs in particular, and tends to provoke a smile of incredulity and derision. The reason for this incomprehension is that mankind has not yet discovered a cure for this disease. Relief from it is to be found only in the oblivion brought about by wine and in the artificial sleep induced by opium and similar narcotics. Alas, the effects of such medicines are only temporary. After a certain point, instead of alleviating the pain, they only intensify it.

Will anyone ever penetrate the secret of this disease which transcends ordinary experience, this reverberation of the shadow of the mind, which manifests itself in a state of coma like that between death and resurrection, when one is neither asleep nor awake?

I propose to deal with only one case of this disease. It concerned me personally and it so shattered my entire being that I shall never be able to drive the thought of it out of my mind. The evil impression which it left has, to a degree that surpasses human understanding, poisoned my life for all time to come. I said 'poisoned'; I should have said that I have ever since borne, and will bear for ever, the brand-mark of that cautery.

I shall try to set down what I can remember, what has remained in my mind of the sequence of events. I may perhaps be able to draw a general conclusion from it all—but no, that is too much to expect. I may hope to be believed by others or at least to convince myself; for, after all, it does not matter to me whether others believe me or not. My one fear is that tomorrow I may die without having come to know myself. In the course of my life I have discovered that a fearful abyss lies between me and other people and have realised that my best course is to remain silent and keep my thoughts to myself for as long as I can. If I have now made up my mind to write it is only in order to reveal myself to my shadow, that shadow which at this moment is stretched across the wall in the attitude of one devouring with insatiable appetite each word I write. It is for his sake that I wish to make the attempt. Who knows? We may perhaps come to know each other better. Ever since I broke the last ties which held me to the rest of mankind my one desire has been to attain a better knowledge of myself.

Idle thoughts! Perhaps. Yet they torment me more savagely than any reality could do. Do not the rest of mankind who look like me, who appear to have the same needs and the same passions as I, exist only in order to cheat me? Are they not a mere handful of shadows which have come into existence only that they may mock and cheat me? Is not everything that I feel, see and think something entirely imaginary, something utterly different from reality?

I am writing only for my shadow, which is now stretched across the wall in the light of the lamp. I must make myself known to him.

2

IN THIS MEAN WORLD OF WRETCHEDNESS AND MISERY I thought that for once a ray of sunlight had broken upon my life. Alas, it was not sunlight, but a passing gleam, a falling star, which flashed upon me, in the form of a woman—or of an angel. In its light, in the course of a second, of a single moment, I beheld all the wretchedness of my existence and apprehended the glory and splendour of the star. After, that brightness disappeared again in the whirlpool of darkness in which it was bound inevitably to disappear. I was unable to retain that passing gleam.

It is three months—no, it is two months and four days—since I lost her from sight but the memory of those magic eyes, of the fatal radiance of those eyes, has remained with me at all times. How can I forget her, who is so intimately bound up with my own existence?

No, I shall never utter her name. For now, with her slender, ethereal, misty form, her great, shining, wondering eyes, in the depths of which my life has slowly and painfully burned and melted away, she no longer belongs to this mean, cruel world. No, I must not defile her name by contact with earthly things.

After she had gone I withdrew from the company of man, from the company of the stupid and the successful and, in order to forget, took refuge in wine and opium. My life passed, and still passes, within the four walls of my room. All my life has passed within four walls.

I used to work through the day, decorating the covers of pen cases. Or, rather, I spent on my trade of pen-case decorator the time that I did not devote to wine and opium. I had chosen this ludicrous trade of pen-case decorator only in order to stupefy myself, in order somehow or other to kill time.

I am fortunate in that the house where I live is situated beyond the edge of the city in a quiet district far from the noise and bustle of life. It is completely isolated and around it lie ruins. Only on the far side of the gully one can see a number of squat mud-brick houses which mark the extreme limit of the city. They must have been built by some fool or madman heaven knows how long ago. When I shut my eyes not only can I see every detail of their structure but I seem to feel the weight of them pressing on my shoulders. They are the sort of houses which one finds depicted only on the covers of ancient pen cases.

I am obliged to set all this down on paper in order to disentangle the various threads of my story. I am obliged to explain it all for the benefit of my shadow on the wall.

Yes, in the past only one consolation, and that a poor one, remained to me. Within the four walls of my room I painted my pictures on the pen cases and thereby, thanks to this ludicrous occupation of mine, managed to get through the day. But when once I had seen those two eyes, once I had seen her, activity of any sort lost all meaning, all content, all value for me.

I would mention a strange, an incredible thing. For some reason unknown to me the subject of all my painting was from the very beginning one and the same. It consisted always of a cypress tree at the foot of which was squatting a bent old man like an Indian fakir. He had a long cloak wrapped about him and wore a turban on his head. The index finger of his left hand was pressed to his lips in a gesture of surprise. Before him stood a girl in a long black dress, leaning towards him and offering him a flower of morning glory. Between them ran a little stream. Had I seen the subject of this picture at some time in the past or had it been revealed to me in a dream? I do not know. What I do know is that whenever I sat down to paint I reproduced the same design, the same subject. My hand independently of my will always depicted the same scene. Strangest of all, I found customers for these paintings of mine. I even despatched some of my pen-case covers to India through the intermediary of my paternal uncle, who used to sell them and remit the money to me.

Somehow I always felt this subject to be remote and, at the same time, curiously familiar to me. I don't remember very well. . . . It occurs to me that I once said to myself that I must write down what I remember of all this—but that happened much later and has nothing to do with the subject of my painting. Moreover, one consequence of this experience was that I gave up painting altogether. That was two months, or, rather exactly, two months and four days ago.

It was the thirteenth day of Nouruz.* Everyone had gone out to the country. I had shut the window of my room in order to be able to concentrate on my painting. It was not long before sunset and I was working away when suddenly the door opened and my uncle came into the room. That is, he said he was my uncle. I had never seen my uncle in my life, for he had been abroad ever since his early youth. I seem to remember that he was a sea captain. I imagined he might have some business matter to discuss with me, since I understood that he was interested in commerce as well. At all events my uncle was a bent old man with an Indian turban on his head and a ragged yellow cloak on his back; his face was partly concealed by a scarf wrapped around

*The national festival of Iran. It begins on March 21 and lasts for thirteen days. It is the custom to spend the last day of Nouruz picnicking in the country.

his neck; his shirt was open and revealed a hairy chest. It would have been possible to count the hairs of the sparse beard protruding from under the scarf which muffled his neck. His eyelids were red and sore and he had a harelip. He resembled me in a remote, comical way like a reflection in a distorting mirror. I had always pictured my father something like this. On entering the room he walked straight across to the opposite wall and squatted on the floor. It occurred to me that I ought to offer him some refreshment in honour of his arrival. I lit the lamp and went into the little dark closet which opens off my room. I searched every corner in the hope of finding something suitable to offer him, although I knew there was nothing of the sort in the house—I had no opium or drink left. Suddenly my eye lighted on the topmost of the shelves on the wall. It was as though I had had a flash of inspiration. On the shelf stood a bottle of old wine which had been left me by my parents. I seem to remember hearing that it had been laid down on the occasion of my birth. There it was on the top shelf. I had never so much as given it a thought and had quite forgotten there was such a thing in the house. To reach the shelf I got up onto a stool which happened to be there. As I reached towards the bottle, I chanced to look out through the ventilation hole above the shelf. On the open ground outside my room I saw a bent old man sitting at the foot of a cypress tree with a young girl—no, an angel from heaven—standing before him. She was leaning forward and with her right hand was offering him a blue flower of morning glory. The old man was biting the nail of the index finger of his left hand.

The girl was directly opposite me but she appeared to be quite unaware of her surroundings. She was gazing straight ahead without looking at anything in particular. She wore on her lips a vague, involuntary smile as though she was thinking of someone who was absent. It was then that I first beheld those frightening, magic eyes, those eyes which seemed to express a bitter reproach to mankind, with their look of anxiety and wonder, of menace and promise—and the current of my existence was drawn towards those shining eyes charged with manifold significance and sank into their depths. That magnetic mirror drew my entire being towards it with inconceivable force. They were slanting, Turkoman eyes of supernatural, intoxicating radiance which at once frightened and attracted, as though they had looked upon terrible, transcendental things which it was given to no one but her to see. Her cheekbones were prominent and her forehead high. Her eyebrows were slender and met in the middle. Her lips were full and half-open as though they had broken away only a moment before from a long, passionate kiss and were not yet sated. Her face, pale as the moon, was framed in the mass of her black, dishevelled hair and one strand clung to her temple. The fineness of her limbs and the ethereal unconstraint of her movements marked her as one who was not fated to live long in this world. No one but a Hindu temple dancer could have possessed her harmonious grace of movement.

Her air of mingled gaiety and sadness set her apart from ordinary mankind. Her beauty was extraordinary. She reminded me of a vision seen in an opium sleep. She aroused in me a heat of passion like that which is kindled by the mandrake root. It seemed to me as I gazed at her long, slender form, with its harmonious lines of shoulder, arms, breasts, waist, buttocks and legs, that she had been torn from her husband's embrace, that she was like the female mandrake which has been plucked from the arms of its mate.

She was wearing a black pleated dress which clung tightly to her body. Gazing at her, I was certain that she wished to leap across the stream which separated her from the old man but that she was unable to do so. All at once the old man burst into laughter. It was a hollow, grating laugh, of a quality to make the hairs of one's body stand on end; a harsh, sinister, mocking laugh. And yet the expression of his face did not change. It was as though the laughter was echoing from somewhere deep within his body.

In terror I sprang down from the stool with the bottle in my hand. I was trembling, in a state of mingled horror and delight such as might have been produced by some delicious, fearful dream. I set the bottle of wine down on the floor and held my head in my hands. How many minutes, how many hours I remained thus, I do not know. When I came to myself I picked up the bottle and went back into my room. My uncle had gone and had left the room door agape like the mouth of a dead man. The sound of the old man's hollow laughter was still echoing in my ears.

It was growing dark. The lamp was burning smokily. I could still feel the aftermath of the delicious, horrible fit of trembling which I had experienced. From that moment the course of my life had changed. With one glance that angel of heaven, that ethereal girl, had left on me the imprint of her being, more deeply marked than the mind of man can conceive.

At that moment I was in a state of trance. It seemed to me that I had long known her name. The radiance of her eyes, her complexion, her perfume, her movements, all appeared familiar to me, as though, in some previous existence in a world of dreams, my soul had lived side by side with hers, had sprung from the same root and the same stock and it was inevitable that we should be brought together again. It was inevitable that I should be close to her in this life. At no time did I desire to touch her. The invisible rays which emanated from our bodies and mingled together were sufficient contact. As for the strange fact that she appeared familiar to me from the first glance, do not lovers always experience the feeling that they have seen each other before and that a mysterious bond has long existed between them? The only thing in this mean world which I desired was her love; if that were denied me I wanted the love of nobody. Was it possible that anyone other than she should make any impression upon my heart? But the hollow grating laughter, the sinister laughter of the old man had broken the bond which united us.

All that night I thought about these things. Again and again I was on the point of going to look through the aperture in the wall, but fear of the old man's laughter held me back. The next day also I could think of nothing else. Would I be able to refrain altogether from going to look at her? Finally on the third day I decided, despite the dread which possessed me, to put the bottle of wine back in its place. But when I drew the curtain aside and looked into the closet I saw in front of me a wall as blank and dark as the darkness which has enshrouded my life. There was no trace of aperture or window. The rectangular opening had been filled in, had merged with the wall, as though it had never existed. I stood upon the stool but, although I hammered on the wall with my fists, listening intently, although I held the lamp to it and examined it with care, there was not the slightest trace of any aperture. My blows had no more effect upon the solid, massive fabric of the wall than if it had been a single slab of lead.

Could I abandon the hope of ever seeing her again? It was not within my power to do so. Henceforth I lived like a soul in torment. All my waiting, watching and seeking were in vain. I trod every handsbreadth of ground in the neighbourhood of my house. I was like the murderer who returns to the scene of his crime. Not one day, not two days, but every day for two months and four days I circled around our house in the late afternoon like a decapitated fowl. I came to know every stone and every pebble in the neighbourhood but I found no trace of the cypress tree, of the little stream or of the two people whom I had seen there. The same number of nights I knelt upon the ground in the moonlight, I begged and entreated the trees, the stones and the moon—for she might have been gazing at that moment at the moon—I sought aid from every created thing, but I found no trace of her. In the end I understood that all my efforts were useless, because it was not possible that she should be connected in any way with the things of this world: the water with which she washed her hair came from some unique, unknown spring; her dress was not woven of ordinary stuff and had not been fashioned by material, human hands. She was a creature apart. I realised that those flowers of morning glory were no ordinary flowers. I was certain that if her face were to come into contact with ordinary water it would fade; and that if she were to pluck an ordinary flower of morning glory with her long fine fingers they would wither like the petals of a flower.

I understood all this. This girl, this angel, was for me a source of wonder and ineffable revelation. Her being was subtle and intangible. She aroused in me a feeling of adoration. I felt sure that beneath the glance of a stranger, of an ordinary man, she would have withered and crumpled.

Ever since I had lost her, ever since the aperture had been blocked and I had been separated from her by a heavy wall, a dank barrier as massive as a wall of lead, I felt that my existence had become pointless, that I had lost my way for all time to come. Even though the caress of her gaze and the profound delight I had experienced in seeing her had been only momentary and devoid of reciprocity—for she had not seen me—yet I felt the need of those eyes. One glance from her would have been sufficient to make plain all the problems of philosophy and the riddles of theology. One glance from her and mysteries and secrets would no longer have existed for me.

From this time on I increased my doses of wine and opium, but alas, those remedies of despair failed to numb and paralyse my mind. I was unable to forget. On the contrary, day by day, hour by hour, minute by minute, the memory of her, of her body, of her face, took shape in my mind more clearly than before.

How could I have forgotten her? Whether my eyes were open or closed, whether I slept or woke, she was always before me. Through the opening in the closet wall, like the dark night which enshrouds the mind and reason of man, through the rectangular aperture which looked onto the outside world, she was ever before my eyes.

Repose was utterly denied me. How could I have found repose?

It had become a habit with me to go out for a walk every day just before sunset. For some obscure reason I wanted desperately to find the little stream, the cypress tree and the vine of morning glory. I had become addicted to these walks in the same way as I had become addicted to opium. It was as though I was compelled by some outside force to undertake them. Throughout my walk I would be immersed in the thought of her, in the memory of my first glimpse of her, and I desired to find the place where I had seen her on that thirteenth day of Nouruz: if I should find that place, if it should be granted to me to sit beneath that cypress tree, then for sure I should attain peace. But alas, there was nothing but sweepings, burning sand, horse bones and refuse heaps around which dogs were sniffing. Had I ever really encountered her? Never. All that had happened was that I had looked furtively, covertly at her through a hole, a cursed aperture in my closet wall. I was like a hungry dog sniffing and rooting in a refuse heap: when people come to dump garbage on the pile he runs away and hides, only to return later to renew his search for tasty morsels. This was the state that I was in. But the aperture in the wall was blocked. For me the girl was like a bunch of fresh flowers which had been tossed onto a refuse heap.

On the last evening when I went out for my usual walk, the sky was overcast and a drizzling rain was falling. A dense mist had fallen over the surrounding country. In the fine rain which softened the intensity of the colours and the clarity of the outlines I experienced a sense of liberation and tranquillity. It was as though the rain was washing away my black thoughts. That night what ought not to have happened did happen.

I wandered, unconscious of my surroundings. During those hours of solitude, during those minutes which lasted I know not how long, her awe-inspiring face, indistinct as though seen through cloud or mist, void of motion or expression like the paintings one sees upon the covers of pen cases, took shape before my eyes far more clearly than ever before.

By the time I returned home I should think that a great part of the night was spent. The mist had grown denser, so much so that I could not see the ground immediately in front of my foot. Nevertheless, by force of habit and some special sense which I had developed, I found my way back to the house. As I came up to the entrance I observed a female form clad in black sitting on the stone bench outside the door.

I struck a match to find the keyhole and for some reason glanced involuntarily at the figure in black. I recognised two slanting eyes, two great black eyes set in a thin face of moonlight paleness, two eyes which gazed unseeing at my face. If I had never seen her before I should still have known her. No, it was not an illusion. This black-robed form was she. I stood bemused, like a man dreaming, who knows that he is dreaming and wishes to awake but cannot. I was unable to move. The match burned down and scorched my fingers. I abruptly came to myself and turned the key in the lock. The door opened and I stood aside. She rose from the bench and passed along the dark corridor like one who knew the way. She opened my door and I followed her into the room. I hurriedly lit the lamp and saw that she had gone across and lain down upon my bed. Her face was in shadow. I did not know whether or not she could see me, whether or not she could hear my voice. She seemed neither to be afraid nor to be inclined to resist. It was as though she had come to my room independently of any will of her own.

Was she ill? Had she lost her way? She had come like a sleepwalker, independently of any will of her own. No one can possibly imagine the sensations I experienced at that moment. I felt a kind of delicious, ineffable pain. No, it was not an illusion. This being who without surprise and without a word had come into my room was that woman, that girl. I had always imagined that our first meeting would be like this. My state of mind was that of a man in an infinitely deep sleep. One must be plunged in profound sleep in order to behold such a dream as this. The silence had for me the force of eternal life; for on the plane of eternity without beginning and without end there is no such thing as speech.

To me she was a woman and at the same time had within her something that transcended humanity. When I looked at her face I experienced a kind of vertigo which made me forget the faces of all other people. Gazing at her, I began to tremble all over and my knees felt weak. In the depths of her immense eyes I beheld in one moment all the wretchedness of my life. Her eyes were wet and shining like two huge black diamonds suffused with tears. In her eyes, her black eyes, I found the everlasting night of impenetrable darkness for which I had been seeking and I sank into the awful, enchanted blackness of that abyss. It was as though she was drawing some faculty out of my being. The ground rocked beneath my feet and if I had fallen I should have experienced an ineffable delight.

My heart stood still. I held my breath. I was afraid that if I breathed she might disappear like cloud or smoke. Her silence seemed something supernatural. It was as though a wall of crystal had risen between her and me, and that second, that hour or that eternity was suffocating me. Her eyes, weary perhaps with looking upon some supernatural sight which it is not given to other people to see, perhaps upon death itself, slowly closed. Her eyelids closed and I, feeling like a drowning man who after frantic struggle and effort has reached the surface of the water, realised that I was feverish and trembling and with the edge of my sleeve wiped away the sweat that was streaming from my forehead.

Her face preserved the same stillness, the same tranquil expression, but seemed to have grown thinner and frailer. As she lay there on my bed she was biting the nail of the index finger of her left hand. Her complexion was pale as the moon and her thin, clinging black dress revealed the lines of her legs, her arms, her breasts—of her whole body.

I leaned over her in order to see her more plainly. Her eyes were closed. However much I might gaze at her face, she still seemed infinitely remote from me. All at once I felt that I had no knowledge of the secrets of her heart and that no bond existed between us.

I wished to say something but I feared that my voice would offend her ears, her sensitive ears which were accustomed, surely, to distant, heavenly, gentle music.

It occurred to me that she might be hungry or thirsty. I went into the closet to look for something to give her, although I knew there was nothing in the house. Then it was as though I had had a flash of inspiration. I remembered that on the top shelf was a bottle of old wine which had been left to me by my father. I got up onto a stool and took it down. I walked across on tip-toe to the bed. She was sleeping like a weary child. She was sound asleep and her long, velvety eyelashes were closed. I opened the bottle and slowly and carefully poured a glassful of the wine into her mouth between the two locked rows of teeth.

Quite suddenly, for the first time in my life, a sensation of peace took possession of me. As I looked upon those closed eyes it was as though the demon which had been torturing me, the incubus which had been oppressing my heart with its iron paw, had fallen asleep for a while. I brought my chair to the side of the bed and gazed fixedly at her face. What a childlike face it was! What an unworldly expression it wore! Was it possible that this woman, this girl or this angel of hell (for I did not know by what name to call her), was it possible that she should possess this double nature? She was so peaceful, so unconstrained!

I could now feel the warmth of her body and smell the odour of dampness that rose from her black, heavy tresses. For some reason unknown to me I raised my trembling hand—my hand was not under my control—and laid it upon a strand of her hair, that lock which always clung to her temple. Then I thrust my fingers into her hair. It was cold and damp. Cold, utterly cold. It was as though she had been dead for several days. I was not mistaken. She *was* dead. I inserted my hand into the front of her dress and laid it upon her breast above the heart. There was not the faintest beat. I took a mirror and held it before her nostrils, but no trace of life remained in her.

I thought that I might be able to warm her with the heat of my own body, to give my warmth to her and to receive in exchange the coldness of death; perhaps in this way I could infuse my spirit into her dead body. I undressed and lay down beside her on the bed. We were locked together like the male and female of the mandrake. Her body was like that of a female mandrake which had been torn apart from its mate and she aroused the same burning passion as the mandrake. Her mouth was acrid and bitter and tasted like the stub end of a cucumber. Her whole body was as cold as hail. I felt that the blood had frozen in my veins and that this cold penetrated to the depths of my heart. All my efforts were useless. I got off the bed and put on my clothes. No, it was not an illusion. She had come here, into my room, into my bed and had surrendered her body to me. She had given me her body and her soul.

So long as she lived, so long as her eyes overflowed with life, I had been tortured by the mere memory of her eyes. Now, inanimate and still, cold, with her eyes closed, she had surrendered herself to me—with her eyes closed.

This was she who had poisoned my whole life from the moment that I first saw her—unless my nature was such that from the beginning it was destined to be poisoned and any other mode of existence was impossible for me. Now, here, in my room, she had yielded to me her body and her shadow. Her fragile, short-lived spirit, which had no affinity with the world of earthly creatures, had silently departed from under the black, pleated dress, from the body which had tormented it, and had gone wandering in the world of shadows and I felt as though it had taken my spirit with it. But her body was lying there, inanimate and still. Her soft, relaxed muscles, her veins and sinews and bones were awaiting burial, a dainty meal for the worms and rats of the grave. In this threadbare, wretched, cheerless room which itself was like a tomb, in the darkness of the everlasting night which had enveloped me and which had penetrated the very fabric of the walls, I had before me a long, dark, cold endless night in the company of a corpse, of her corpse. I felt that ever since the world had been the world, so long as I had lived, a corpse, cold, inanimate and still, had been with me in a dark room.

At that moment my thoughts were numbed. Within me I felt a new and singular form of life. My being was somehow connected with that of all the creatures that existed about me, with all the shadows that quivered around me. I was in intimate, inviolable communion with the outside world and with all created things, and a complex system of invisible conductors transmitted a restless flow of impulses between me and all the elements of nature. There was no conception, no notion which I felt to be foreign to me. I was capable of penetrating with ease the secrets of the painters of the past, the mysteries of abstruse philosophies, the ancient folly of ideas and species. At that moment I participated in the revolutions of earth and heaven, in the germination of plants and in the instinctive movements of animals. Past and future, far and near had joined together and fused in the life of my mind.

At such times as this every man takes refuge in some firmly established habit, in his own particular passion. The drunkard stupefies himself with drink, the writer writes, the sculptor attacks the stone. Each relieves his mind of the burden by recourse to his own stimulant and it is at such times as this that the real artist is capable of producing a masterpiece. But I, listless and helpless as I was, I, the decorator of pen-case covers, what could I do? What means had I of creating a masterpiece when all that I could make were my lifeless, shiny little pictures, each of them identical with all the rest? And yet in my whole being I felt an overflowing enthusiasm, an indescribable warmth of inspiration. I desired to record on paper those eyes which had closed forever; I would keep the picture by me always. The force of this desire compelled me to translate it into action. I could not resist the impulsion. How could I have resisted it, I, an artist shut up in a room with a dead body? The thought aroused in me a peculiar sensation of delight.

I extinguished the smoky lamp, brought a pair of candles, lighted them and set them above her head. In the flickering candlelight her face was still more tranquil than before; in the half-dark of the room it wore an expression of mystery and immateriality. I fetched paper and the other things necessary for my task and took up my position beside her bed—for henceforth the bed was hers. My intention was to portray at my leisure this form which was doomed slowly and gradually to suffer decomposition and disintegration and which now lay still, a fixed expression upon its face. I felt that I must record on paper its essential lines. I would select those lines of which I had myself experienced the power. A painting, even though it be summary and unpretentious, must nevertheless produce an emotional effect and possess a kind of life. I, however, was accustomed only to executing a stereotyped pattern on the covers of pen cases. I had now to bring my own mind into play, to give concrete form to an image which existed in my mind, that image which, emanating from her face, had so impressed itself upon all my thoughts. I would glance once at her face and shut my eyes. Then I would set down on paper the lines which I had selected for my purpose. Thereby I hoped to create from the resources of my mind a drug which would soothe my tortured spirit. I was taking refuge in the end in the motionless life of lines and forms.

The subject I had chosen, a dead woman, had a curious affinity to my dead manner of painting. I had never been anything else than a painter of dead bodies. And now I was faced with the question: was it necessary for me to see her eyes again, those eyes which were now closed? Or were they already imprinted upon my memory with sufficient clarity?

I do not know how many times I drew and redrew her portrait in the course of that night, but none of my pictures satisfied me and I tore them up as fast as I painted them. The work did not tire me and I did not notice the passage of time.

The darkness was growing thin and the windowpanes admitted a grey light into my room. I was busy with a picture which seemed to me to be better than any of the others. But the eyes? Those eyes, with their expression of reproach as though they had seen me commit some unpardonable sin—I was incapable of depicting them on paper. The image of those eyes seemed suddenly to have been effaced from my memory. All my efforts were useless. However much I might study her face, I was unable to bring their expression to mind.

All at once as I looked at her a flush began to appear upon her cheeks. They gradually were suffused with a crimson colour like that of the meat that hangs in front of butchers' shops. She returned to life. Her feverish, reproachful eyes, shining with a hectic brilliance, slowly opened and gazed fixedly at my face. It was the first time she had been conscious of my presence, the first time she had looked at me. Then the eyes closed again.

The thing probably lasted no more than a moment but this was enough for me to remember the expression of her eyes and to set it down on paper. With the tip of my paintbrush I recorded that expression and this time I did not tear up my picture.

Then I stood up and went softly to the bedside. I supposed that she was alive, that she had come back to life, that my love had infused life into her dead body. But at close quarters I detected the corpse smell, the smell of a corpse in process of decomposition. Tiny maggots were wriggling on her body and a pair of blister-flies were circling in the light of the candles. She was quite dead. But why, how, had her eyes opened? Had it been a hallucination or had it really happened?

I prefer not to be asked this question. But the essential was her face, or, rather, her eyes—and now they were in my possession. I had fixed on paper the spirit which had inhabited those eyes and I had no further need of the body, that body which was doomed to disappear, to become the prey of the worms and rats of the grave. Henceforth she was in my power and I had ceased to be her creature. I could see her eyes whenever I felt inclined to do so. I took up my picture as carefully as I could, laid it in a tin box which served me as a safe and put the box away in the closet behind my room.

The night was departing on tip-toe. One felt that it had shed sufficient of its weariness to enable it to go its way. The ear detected faint, far-off sounds such as the sprouting grass might have made, or some migratory bird as it dreamed upon the wing. The pale stars were disappearing behind banks of cloud. I felt the gentle breath of the morning on my face and at the same moment a cock crowed somewhere in the distance.

What was I to do with the body, a body which had already begun to decompose? At first I thought of burying it in my room, then of taking it away and throwing it down some well surrounded by flowers of blue morning glory. But how much thought, how much effort and dexterity would be necessary in order to do these things without attracting attention! And then, I did not want the eye of any stranger to fall upon her. I had to do everything alone and unaided. Not that I mattered. What point was there to my existence now that she had gone? But she—never, never must any ordinary person, anyone but me, look upon her dead body. She had come to my room and had surrendered her cold body and her shadow to me in order that no one else should see her, in order that she should not be defiled by a stranger's glance. Finally an idea came to me. I would cut up her body, pack it in a suitcase, my old suitcase, take it away with me to some place far, very far from people's eyes, and bury it there.

This time I did not hesitate. I took a bone-handled knife that I kept in the closet beside my room and began by cutting open with great care the dress of fine black material which swathed her like a spider's web. It was the only covering she wore on her body. She seemed to have grown a little: her body appeared to be longer than it had been in life. Then I severed the head. Drops of cold clotted blood trickled from her neck. Next, I amputated the arms and legs. I neatly fitted the trunk along with the head and limbs into the suitcase and covered the whole with her dress, the same black dress. I locked the case and put the key into my pocket. When I had finished I drew a deep breath of relief and tried the weight of the suitcase. It was heavy. Never before had I experienced such overwhelming weariness. No, I should never be able to remove the suitcase on my own.

The weather had again set to mist and fine rain. I went outside in the hope of finding someone who might help me with the case. There was not a soul to be seen. I walked a little way, peering into the mist. Suddenly I caught sight of a bent old man sitting at the foot of a cypress tree. His face could not be seen for a wide scarf which he wore wrapped around his neck. I walked slowly up to him. I had still not uttered a word when the old man burst into a hollow, grating, sinister laugh which made the hairs on my body stand on end and said,

'If you want a porter, I'm at your service. Yes. I've got a hearse as well. I take dead bodies every day to Shah Abdo'l-Azim* and bury them there. Yes. I make coffins, too. Got coffins of every size, the perfect fit for everybody. At your service. Right away.'

He roared with laughter, so that his shoulders shook. I pointed in the direction of my house but he said, before I had a chance to utter a word,

'That's all right. I know where you live. I'll be there right away.'

He stood up and I walked back to my house. I went into my room and with difficulty got the suitcase with the dead body across to the door. I observed, standing in the street outside the door, a dilapidated old hearse to which were harnessed two black, skeleton-thin horses. The bent old man was sitting on the driver's seat at the front of the hearse, holding a long whip. He did not turn to look in my direction. With a great effort I heaved the suitcase into the hearse, where there was a sunken space designed to hold the coffins, after which I climbed on board myself and lay down in the coffin space, resting my head against the ledge

*A mosque and cemetery situated among the ruins of Rey, a few miles south of Teheran. Rey (the Rhages of the Greeks) was an important center from at least the eighth century B.C. and continued to be one of the great cities of Iran down to its destruction by Genghis Khan in the thirteenth century A.D.

so as to be able to see out as we drove along. I slid the suitcase onto my chest and held it firmly with both hands.

The whip whistled through the air; the horses set off, breathing hard. The vapour could be seen through the drizzling rain, rising from their nostrils like a stream of smoke. They moved with high, smooth paces. Their thin legs, which made me think of the arms of a thief whose fingers have been cut off in accordance with the law and the stumps plunged into boiling oil, rose and fell slowly and made no sound as they touched the ground. The bells around their necks played a strange tune in the damp air. A profound sensation of comfort to which I can assign no cause penetrated me from head to foot and the movement of the hearse did not impart itself in any degree to my body. All that I could feel was the weight of the suitcase upon my chest. I felt as if the weight of her dead body and the coffin in which it lay had for all time been pressing upon my chest.

The country on each side of the road was enveloped in dense mist. With extraordinary speed and smoothness the hearse passed by hills, level ground and streams, and a new and singular landscape unfolded before me, one such as I had never seen, sleeping or waking. On each side of the road was a line of hills standing quite clear of one another. At the foot of the hills there were numbers of weird, crouching, accursed trees, between which one caught sight of ash-grey houses shaped like pyramids, cubes and prisms, with low, dark windows without panes. The windows were like the wild eyes of a man in a state of delirium. The walls of the houses appeared to possess the property of instilling intense cold into the heart of the passerby. One felt that no living creature could ever have dwelt in those houses. Perhaps they had been built to house the ghosts of ethereal beings.

Apparently the driver of the hearse was taking me by a byroad or by some special route of his own. In some places all that was to be seen on either side of the road were stumps and wry, twisted trees, beyond which were houses, some squat, some tall, of geometrical shapes—perfect cones, truncated cones—with narrow, crooked windows from which blue flowers of morning glory protruded and twined over the doors and walls. Then this landscape disappeared abruptly in the dense mist.

The heavy, pregnant clouds which covered the tops of the hills sagged oppressively. The wind was blowing up a fine rain like aimless, drifting dust. We had been travelling for a considerable time when the hearse stopped at the foot of a stony, arid hill on which there was no trace of greenery. I slid the suitcase off my chest and got out.

On the other side of the hill was an isolated enclosure, peaceful and green. It was a place which I had never seen before and yet it looked familiar to me, as though it had always been present in some recess of my mind. The ground was covered with vines of blue, scentless morning glory. I felt that no one until that moment had ever set foot in the place. I pulled the suitcase out and set it down on the ground. The old driver turned round and said,

'We're not far from Shah Abdo'l Azim. You won't find a better place than this for what you want. There's never a bird flies by here. No.'

I put my hand into my pocket, intending to pay the driver his fare. All that I had with me were two *krans* and one *abbasi.** The driver burst into a hollow, grating laugh and said,

'That's all right. Don't bother. I'll get it from you later. I know where you live. You haven't got any other jobs for me, no? I know something about grave digging, I can tell you. Yes. Nothing to be ashamed of. Shall we go? There's a stream near here, by a cypress tree. I'll dig you a hole just the right size for the suitcase and then we'll go.'

The old man sprang down from his seat with a nimbleness of which I could not have imagined him to be capable. I took up the case and we walked side by side until we reached a dead tree which stood beside a dry riverbed. My companion said,

'This is a good place.'

Without waiting for an answer, he began at once to dig with a small spade and a pick which he had brought with him. I set the suitcase down and stood beside it in a kind of

*Coins worth respectively 5d. and 1d.

torpor. The old man, bent double, was working away with the deftness of one who was used to the job. In the course of his digging he came across an object which looked like a glazed jar. He wrapped it up in a dirty handkerchief, stood up and said,

'There's your hole. Yes. Just the right size for the suitcase. The perfect fit. Yes.'

I put my hand into my pocket to pay him for his work. All that I had with me were two *krans* and one *abbasi*. The old man burst into a hollow laugh which brought out gooseflesh all over my body and said,

'Don't worry about that. That's all right. I know where you live. Yes. In any case, I found a jar that'll do me instead of pay. It's a flower vase from Rhages, comes from the ancient city of Rey. Yes.'

Then, as he stood there, bent and stooping, he began to laugh again so that his shoulders shook. He tucked the jar, wrapped in the dirty handkerchief, under his arm and walked off to the hearse. With surprising nimbleness he sprang up and took his place on the driver's seat. The whip whistled through the air, the horses set off, breathing hard. The bells around their necks played a strange tune in the damp air. Gradually they disappeared into the dense mist.

As soon as I was alone I breathed a deep breath of relief. I felt as though a heavy weight had been lifted from my chest, and a wonderful sensation of peace permeated my whole being. I looked around me. The place where I stood was a small enclosure surrounded on every side by blue hills and mounds. Along one ridge extended the ruins of ancient buildings constructed of massive bricks. Nearby was a dry riverbed. It was a quiet, remote spot far from the noise and tumult of men. I felt profoundly happy and reflected that those great eyes, when they awoke from the sleep of earth, would behold a place which was in harmony with their own nature and aspect. And at the same time it was fitting that, just as she had been far removed from the life of other people while she was alive, so she should remain far from the rest of mankind, far from the other dead.

I lifted the suitcase with great care and lowered it into the trench, which proved to be of exactly the right dimensions, a perfect fit. However, I felt that I must look into the case once more. I looked around. Not a soul was to be seen. I took the key from my pocket and opened the lid. I drew aside a corner of her black dress and saw, amid a mass of coagulated blood and swarming maggots, two great black eyes gazing fixedly at me with no trace of expression in them. I felt that my entire being was submerged in the depths of those eyes. Hastily I shut the lid of the case and pushed the loose earth in on top of it. When the trench was filled in I trampled the earth firm, brought a number of vines of blue, scentless morning glory and set them in the ground above her grave. Then I collected sand and pebbles and scattered them around in order to obliterate the traces of the burial so completely that nobody should be able to tell that it had ever taken place. I performed this task so well that I myself was unable to distinguish her grave from the surrounding ground.

When I had finished I looked down at myself and saw that my clothes were torn and smeared with clay and black, clotted blood. Two blister-flies were circling around me and a number of tiny maggots were wriggling, stuck to my clothes. In an attempt to remove the bloodstains from the skirts of my coat I moistened the edge of my sleeve with saliva and rubbed at the patches; but the bloodstains only soaked into the material, so that they penetrated through to my body and I felt the clamminess of blood upon my skin.

It was not long before sunset and a fine rain was falling. I began to walk and involuntarily followed the wheel tracks of the hearse. When night came on I lost the tracks but continued to walk on in the profound darkness, slowly and aimlessly, with no conscious thought in my mind, like a man in a dream. I had no idea in what direction I was going. Since she had gone, since I had seen those great eyes amid a mass of coagulated blood, I had felt that I was walking in a profound darkness which had completely enshrouded my life. Those eyes which had been a lantern lighting my way had been extinguished forever and now I did not care whether or not I ever arrived at any place.

There was complete silence everywhere. I felt that all mankind had rejected me and I took refuge with inanimate things. I was conscious of a relationship between me and the pulsation of nature, between me and the profound night which had descended upon my spirit. This silence is a language which we do not understand. My head began to swim, in a kind of intoxication. A sensation of nausea came over me and my legs felt weak. I experienced a sense of infinite weariness. I went into a cemetery beside the road and sat down upon a gravestone. I held my head between my hands and tried to think steadily of the situation I was in.

Suddenly I was brought to myself by the sound of a hollow grating laugh. I turned and saw a figure with its face concealed by a scarf muffled around its neck. It was seated beside me and held under its arm something wrapped in a handkerchief. It turned to me and said,

'I suppose you want to get into town? Lost your way, eh? Suppose you're wondering what I'm doing in a graveyard at this time of night? No need to be afraid. Dead bodies are my regular business. Grave digging's my trade. Not a bad trade, eh? I know every nook and cranny of this place. Take a case in point—today I went out on a grave-digging job. Found this jar in the ground. Know what it is? It's a flower vase from Rhages, comes from the ancient city of Rey. Yes. That's all right, you can have the jar. Keep it to remember me by.'

I put my hand into my pocket and took out two *krans* and one *abbasi*. The old man, with a hollow laugh which brought out gooseflesh all over my body, said,

'No, no. That's all right. I know you. Know where you live, too. I've got a hearse standing just near here. Come and I'll drive you home. Yes. It's only two steps away.'

He put the jar into my lap and stood up. He was laughing so violently that his shoulders shook. I picked up the jar and set off in the wake of the stooping figure. By a bend in the road was standing a ramshackle hearse with two gaunt black horses harnessed to it. The old man sprang up with surprising nimbleness and took his place on the driver's seat. I climbed onto the vehicle and stretched myself out in the sunken space where they put the coffins, resting my head against the high ledge so that I should be able to look out as we drove along. I laid the jar on my chest and held it in place with my hand.

The whip whistled through the air; the horses set off, breathing hard. They moved with high, smooth paces. Their hoofs touched the ground gently and silently. The bells around their necks played a strange tune in the damp air. In the gaps between the clouds the stars gazed down at the earth like gleaming eyes emerging from a mass of coagulated blood. A wonderful sense of tranquillity pervaded my whole being. All that I could feel was the jar pressing against my chest with the weight of a dead body. The interlocking trees with their wry, twisted branches seemed in the darkness to be gripping one another by the hand for fear they should slip and crash to the ground. The sides of the road were lined with weird houses of individual geometrical shapes, with forlorn, black windows. The walls of the houses, like glowworms, gave forth a dim, sickly radiance. The trees passed by alarmingly in clumps and in rows and fled away from us. But it appeared to me that their feet became entangled in vines of morning glory which brought them to the ground. The smell of death, the smell of decomposing flesh, pervaded me, body and soul. It seemed to me that I had always been saturated with the smell of death and had slept all my life in a black coffin while a bent old man whose face I could not see transported me through the mist and the passing shadows.

The hearse stopped. I picked up the jar and sprang to the ground. I was outside the door of my own house. I hurriedly went in and entered my room. I put the jar down on the table, went straight into the closet and brought out from its hiding place the tin box which served me as a safe. I went to the door, intending to give it to the old hearse-driver in lieu of payment, but he had disappeared; there was no sign of him or of his hearse. Frustrated, I went back to my room. I lit the lamp, took the jar out of the handkerchief in which it was wrapped and with my sleeve rubbed away the earth which coated it. It was an ancient vase with a transparent violet glaze which had turned to the colour of a crushed blister-fly. On one side of the belly of the vase was an almond-shaped panel framed in blue flowers of morning glory, and in the panel . . .

In the almond-shaped panel was *her* portrait . . . the face of a woman with great black eyes, eyes that were bigger than other people's. They wore a look of reproach, as though they had seen me commit some inexpiable sin of which I had no knowledge. They were frightening, magic eyes with an expression of anxiety and wonder, of menace and promise. They terrified me and attracted me and an intoxicating, supernatural radiance shone from their depths. Her cheekbones were prominent and her forehead high. Her eyebrows were slender and met in the middle. Her lips were full and half-open. Her hair was dishevelled, and one strand of it clung to her temple.

I took out from the tin box the portrait I had painted of her the night before and compared the two. There was not an atom of difference between my picture and that on the jar. The one might have been the reflection of the other in a mirror. The two were identical and were, it seemed obvious, the work of one man, one ill-fated decorator of pen cases. Perhaps the soul of the vase-painter had taken possession of me when I made my portrait and my hand had followed his guidance. It was impossible to tell the two apart, except that my picture was on paper while the painting on the vase was covered with an ancient transparent glaze which gave it a mysterious air, a strange, supernatural air. In the depths of the eyes burned a spark of the spirit of evil. No, the thing was past belief: both pictures depicted the same great eyes, void of thought, the same reserved yet unconstrained expression of face. It is impossible to imagine the sensations that arose in me. I wished that I could run away from myself. Was such a coincidence conceivable? All the wretchedness of my life rose again before my eyes. Was it not enough that in the course of my life I should encounter one person with such eyes as these? And now two people were gazing at me from the same eyes, *her* eyes. The thing was beyond endurance. Those eyes to which I had given burial there, by the hill, at the foot of the dead cypress tree, beside the dry riverbed, under the blue flowers of morning glory, amid thick blood, amid maggots and foul creatures which were holding festival around her, while the plant roots were already reaching down to force their way into the pupils and suck forth their juices—those same eyes, brimful of vigorous life, were at that moment gazing at me.

I had not known that I was ill-starred and accursed to such a degree as this. And yet at the same time the sense of guilt that lurked in my mind gave rise to a strange, inexplicable feeling of comfort. I realised that I had an ancient partner in sorrow. Was not that ancient painter who, hundreds, perhaps thousands, of years ago, had decorated the surface of this jar my partner in sorrow? Had he not undergone the same spiritual experiences as I? Until now I had regarded myself as the most ill-starred of created beings. Now I understood for a space that on those hills, in the houses of that ruined city of massive brick, had once lived men whose bones had long since rotted away and the atoms of whose bodies might now perhaps be living another life in the blue flowers of morning glory; and that among those men there had been one, an unlucky painter, an accursed painter, perhaps an unsuccessful decorator of pen-case covers, who had been a man like me, exactly like me. And now I understood (it was all that I was capable of understanding) that his life also had burned and melted away in the depths of two great black eyes, just as mine had done. The thought gave me consolation.

I set my painting beside that upon the jar and went and kindled the charcoal in my opium brazier. When it was burning well I set the brazier down in front of the two paintings. I drew a few whiffs of the opium pipe and, as the drug began to take effect, gazed steadily at the pictures. I felt that I had to concentrate my thoughts, and the only thing that enabled me to do so and to achieve tranquillity of mind were the ethereal fumes of opium.

I smoked my whole stock of opium, in the hope that the wonder-working drug would resolve the problems that vexed me, draw aside the curtain that hung before the eye of my mind and dispel my accumulation of distant, ashy memories. I attained the spiritual state for which I was waiting and that to a higher degree than I had anticipated. My thoughts acquired the subtlety and grandeur which only opium can confer and I sank into a condition between sleep and coma.

Then I felt as though a heavy weight had been removed from my chest, as though the law of gravity had ceased to exist for me and I soared freely in pursuit of my thoughts, which had grown ample, ingenious and infinitely precise. A profound and ineffable delight took possession of me. I had been released from the burden of my body. My whole being was sinking into the torpor of vegetable existence. The world in which I found myself was a tranquil world, but one filled with enchanted, exquisite forms and colours. Then the thread of my thoughts snapped asunder and dissolved amid the colours and the shapes. I was immersed in a sea, the waves of which bestowed ethereal caresses upon me. I could hear my heart beating, could feel the throbbing of my arteries. It was a state of existence charged with significance and delight.

From the bottom of my heart I desired to surrender myself to the sleep of oblivion. If only oblivion were attainable, if it could last forever, if my eyes as they closed could gently transcend sleep and dissolve into nonbeing and I should lose consciousness of my existence for all time to come, if it were possible for my being to dissolve in one drop of ink, in one bar of music, in one ray of coloured light, and then these waves and forms were to grow and grow to such infinite size that in the end they faded and disappeared—then I should have attained my desire.

Gradually a sensation of numbness took hold of me. It resembled a kind of agreeable weariness. I had the impression that a continuous succession of subtle waves was emanating from my body. Then I felt as though the course of my life had been reversed. One by one past experiences, past states of mind and obliterated, lost memories of childhood recurred to me. Not only did I see these things but I took part in the bustle of bygone activity, was wholly immersed in it. With each moment that passed I grew smaller and more like a child. Then suddenly my mind became blank and dark and it seemed to me that I was suspended from a slender hook in the shaft of a dark well. Then I broke free of the hook and dropped through space. No obstacle interrupted my fall. I was falling into an infinite abyss in an everlasting night. After that a long series of forgotten scenes flashed one after another before my eyes. I experienced a moment of utter oblivion. When I came to myself, I found myself in a small room and in a peculiar posture which struck me as strange and at the same time natural to me.

3

WHEN I AWOKE IN A NEW WORLD EVERYTHING THAT I found there was perfectly familiar and near to me, so much so that I felt more at home in it than in my previous surroundings and manner of life, which, so it seemed to me, had been only the reflection of my real life. It was a different world but one in such perfect harmony with me that I felt as though I had returned to my natural surroundings. I had been born again in a world which was ancient but which at the same time was closer and more natural to me than the other.

It was still twilight. An oil lamp was burning on a shelf. There was a bed unrolled* in the corner of the room, but I was awake. My body felt burning hot. There were bloodstains on my cloak and scarf and my hands were covered with blood. But in spite of fever and giddiness I experienced

*In old Persia bedsteads were not used. The bedroll (mattress, sheet, pillows and quilt) was stowed away in the daytime and unrolled on the floor at night.

a peculiar animation and restlessness which were stronger than any thought I might have had of removing the traces of blood, more powerful than the thought that the police would come and arrest me. In any case I had been expecting for some time to be arrested and had made up my mind, should they come, to gulp down a glass of the poisoned wine which I kept on the top shelf. The source of my excitement was the need to write, which I felt as a kind of obligation imposed on me. I hoped by this means to expel the demon which had long been lacerating my vitals, to vent onto paper the horrors of my mind. Finally, after some hesitation, I drew the oil lamp towards me and began as follows:

4

IT WAS ALWAYS MY OPINION THAT THE BEST COURSE A man could take in life was to remain silent; that one could not do better than withdraw into solitude like the bittern which spreads its wings beside some lonely lake. But now, since that which should not have happened has happened, I cannot help myself. Who knows? Perhaps in the course of the next few moments, perhaps in an hour's time, a band of drunken policemen will come to arrest me. I have not the least desire to save my carcass, and in any case it would be quite impossible for me to deny the crime, even supposing that I could remove the bloodstains. But before I fall into their hands I shall swallow a glass from the bottle of wine, my heirloom, which I keep on the top shelf.

I wish now to squeeze out every drop of juice from my life as from a cluster of grapes and to pour the juice—the wine, rather—drop by drop, like water of Karbala,* down the

*The burial place of the Shia martyr Hosein. Water in which a little earth from Karbala had been steeped was employed as medicine.

parched throat of my shadow. All that I hope to do is to record on paper before I go the torments which have slowly wasted me away like gangrene or cancer here in my little room. This is the best means I have of bringing order and regularity into my thoughts. Is it my intention to draw up a last will and testament? By no means. I have no property for the State to devour, I have no faith for the Devil to take. Moreover, what is there on the face of the earth that could have the slightest value for me? What life I had I have allowed to slip away—I permitted it, I even wanted it, to go—and after I have gone what do I care what happens? It is all the same to me whether anyone reads the scraps of paper I leave behind or whether they remain unread forever and a day. The only thing that makes me write is the need, the overmastering need, at this moment more urgent than ever it was in the past, to create a channel between my thoughts and my unsubstantial self, my shadow, that sinister shadow which at this moment is stretched across the wall in the light of the oil lamp in the attitude of one studying attentively and devouring each word I write. This shadow surely understands better than I do. It is only to him that I can talk properly. It is he who compels me to talk. Only he is capable of knowing me. He surely understands. . . . It is my wish, when I have poured the juice—rather, the bitter wine—of my life down the parched throat of my shadow, to say to him, 'This is my life'.

Whoever saw me yesterday saw a wasted, sickly young man. Today he would see a bent old man with white hair, burnt-out eyes and a harelip. I am afraid to look out of the window of my room or to look at myself in the mirror for everywhere I see my own shadow multiplied indefinitely.

However, in order to explain my life to my stooping shadow, I am obliged to tell a story. Ugh! How many stories about love, copulation, marriage and death already exist, not one of which tells the truth! How sick I am of well-constructed plots and brilliant writing!

I shall try to squeeze out the juice from this cluster of grapes, but whether or not the result will contain the slightest particle of truth I do not yet know. I do not know where I am at this moment, whether the patch of sky above my head and these few spans of ground on which I am sitting belong to Nishapur or to Balkh* or to Benares. I feel sure of nothing in the world.

I have seen so many contradictory things and have heard so many words of different sorts, my eyes have seen so much of the worn-out surface of various objects—the thin, tough rind behind which the spirit is hidden—that now I believe nothing. At this very moment I doubt the existence of tangible, solid things; I doubt clear, manifest truths. If I were to strike my hand against the stone mortar that stands

*A reminiscence of a quatrain of Omar Khayyam:
'Since life passes, whether sweet or bitter,
Since the soul must pass the lips, whether in Nishapur or in Balkh,
Drink wine, for after you and I are gone many a moon
Will pass from old to new, from new to old.'

in the corner of our courtyard and were to ask it, 'Are you real and solid?' and the mortar were to reply , 'Yes', I do not know whether I should take its word or not.

Am I a being separate and apart from the rest of creation? I do not know. But when I looked into the mirror a moment ago I did not recognise myself. No, the old 'I' has died and rotted away, but no barrier, no gulf, exists between it and the new one.

I must tell my story, but I am not sure at what point to start. Life is nothing but a fiction, a mere story. I must squeeze out the juice from the cluster of grapes and pour it spoonful by spoonful down the parched throat of this aged shadow. At what point should I start? All the thoughts which are bubbling in my brain at this moment belong to this passing instant and know nothing of hours, minutes and dates. An incident of yesterday may for me be less significant, less recent, than something that happened a thousand years ago.

Perhaps for the very reason that all the bonds which held me to the world of living people have been broken the memories of the past take shape before my eyes. Past, future, hour, day, month, year—these things are all the same to me. The various phases of childhood and maturity are to me nothing but futile words. They mean something only to ordinary people, to the rabble—yes, that is the word I was looking for—the rabble, whose lives, like the year, have their definite periods and seasons and are cast in the temperate zone of existence. But my life has always known only one season and one state of being. It is as though it had been spent in some frigid zone and in eternal darkness while all the time within me burned a flame which consumed me as the flame consumes the candle.

Within the four walls that form my room, this fortress which I have erected around my life and thoughts, my life has been slowly wasting away like a candle. No, I am wrong. It is like a green log which has rolled to one side of the fireplace and which has been scorched and charred by the flames from the other logs; it has neither burnt away nor remained fresh and green; it has been choked by the smoke and steam from the others.

My room, like all rooms, is built of baked and sun-dried bricks and stands upon the ruins of thousands of ancient houses. Its walls are whitewashed and it has a frieze around it. It is exactly like a tomb. I am capable of occupying my thoughts for hours at a stretch with the slightest details of the life of the room—for example, with a little spider in a crevice of the wall. Ever since I have been confined to my bed people have paid little attention to me.

In the wall there is a horseshoe nail which at one time supported the swinging cradle where my wife and I used to sleep and which since then may have supported the weight of other children. Just below the nail there is a patch where the plaster has swelled and fallen away, and from that patch one can detect the odours from the things and the people which have been in the room in the past. No draught or breeze has ever been able to dispel these dense, clinging, stagnant odours: the smell of sweat, the smell of bygone illnesses, the smell of people's mouths, the smell of feet, the acrid smell of urine, the smell of rancid oil, the smell of decayed straw matting, the smell of burnt omelettes, the smell of fried onions, the smell of medicines, the smell of mallow, the smell of dirty napkins, the smell which you find in the rooms of boys lately arrived at puberty, the vapours which have seeped in from the street and the smells of the dead and dying. All of these odours are still alive and have kept their individuality. There are, besides, many other smells of unknown origins which have left their traces there.

Opening off my room is a dark closet. The room itself has two windows facing out onto the world of the rabble. One of them looks onto our own courtyard, the other onto the street, forming thereby a link between me and the city of Rey, the city which they call the 'Bride of the World', with its thousandfold web of winding streets, its host of squat houses, its schools and its caravanserais. The city which is accounted the greatest city in the world is breathing and living its life there beyond my room. When I close my eyes here in my little room the vague, blurred shadows of the city (of which my mind is at all times aware, whether consciously or not) all take substantial form and rise before me in the shape of pavilions, mosques and gardens.

These two windows are my links with the outside world, the world of the rabble. But on the wall inside my room hangs a mirror in which I look at my face, and in my circumscribed existence that mirror is a more important thing than the world of the rabble-men which has nothing to do with me.

The central feature of the city landscape as seen from my window is a wretched little butcher's shop directly opposite our house. It gets through a total of two sheep per day. I can see the butcher every time I look out of the window. Early each morning a pair of gaunt, consumptive-looking horses are led up to the shop. They have a deep, hollow cough and their emaciated legs terminated by blunt hoofs give one the feeling that their fingers have been cut off in accordance with some barbarous law and the stumps plunged into boiling oil. Each of them has a pair of sheep carcases slung across its back. The butcher raises his greasy hand to his henna-dyed beard and begins by appraising the carcases with a buyer's eye. He selects two of them and feels the weight of their tails with his hand. Finally he lugs them across and hangs them from a hook at the entrance to the shop. The horses set off, breathing hard. The butcher stands by the two bloodstained corpses with their gashed throats and their staring bloody-lidded eyes bulging from the bluish skulls. He pats them and feels the flesh with his fingers. Then he takes a long bone-handled knife and cuts up their bodies with great care, after which he smilingly dispenses the meat to his customers. How much pleasure he derives from all these operations! I am convinced that they give him the most exquisite pleasure, even delight. Every morning at this time the thick-necked yellow dog which has made our district his preserve is there outside the butcher's shop. His head on one side, he gazes regretfully with his innocent eyes at the butcher's hand. That dog also understands. He also knows that the butcher enjoys his work.

A little further away under an archway a strange old man is sitting with an assortment of wares spread out in front of him on a canvas sheet. They include a sickle, two horseshoes, assorted coloured beads, a long-bladed knife, a rat trap, a rusty pair of tongs, part of a writing set, a gap-toothed comb, a spade, and a glazed jar over which he has thrown a dirty handkerchief. I have watched him from behind my window for days, hours and months. He always wears a dirty scarf, a Shuster cloak and an open shirt from which protrude the white hairs on his chest. He has inflamed eyelids which are apparently being eaten away by some stubborn, obtrusive disease. He wears a talisman tied to his arm and he always sits in the same posture. On Thursday evenings he reads aloud from the Koran, revealing his yellow, gappy teeth as he does so. One might suppose that he earned his living by this Koran-reading for I have never seen anyone buy anything from him. It seems to me that this man's face has figured in most of my nightmares. What crass, obstinate ideas have grown up, weed-like, inside that shaven greenish skull under its embroidered turban, behind that low forehead? One feels that the canvas sheet in front of the old man, with its assortment of odds and ends, has some curious affinity to the life of the old man himself. More than once I have made up my mind to go up and exchange a word with him or buy something from his collection, but I have not found the courage to do so.

According to my nurse, the old man was a potter in his younger days. After giving up that trade he kept only this one jar for himself and now he earned his living by peddling.

These were my links with the outside world. Of my private world all that was left to me were my nurse and my bitch of a wife. But Nanny was her nurse too; she was nurse to both of us. My wife and I were not only closely related but were suckled together by Nanny. Her mother was to all intents and purposes mine too because I never saw my parents but was brought up by her mother, a tall, grey-haired woman. I loved her as much as if she had been my real mother, and that was the reason why I married her daughter.

I have heard several different accounts of my father and mother. Only one of them, the one Nanny gave me, can, I imagine, be true. This is what Nanny told me:

My father and my uncle were twins. They resembled each other exactly in figure, face and disposition, and even their voices were identical. So it was no easy matter to tell them apart. Moreover, there existed between them a mental bond or sympathy as a result of which, to take an example, if one of them fell ill the other would fall ill also. In the common phrase, they were like two halves of the one apple.

In due course they both decided to go into commerce and, when they reached the age of twenty, they went off to India, where they opened up a business in Rey wares, including textiles of various kinds—shot silk, flowered stuffs, cotton piece-goods, jubbahs, shawls, needles, earthenware, fuller's earth, and pen-case covers. My father settled in Benares and used to send my uncle on business trips to the other cities of India. After some time, my father fell in love with a girl called Bugam Dasi, a dancer in a lingam temple. Besides performing ritual dances before the great lingam idol she served as a temple attendant. She was a hot-blooded, olive-skinned girl, with lemon-shaped breasts, great, slanting eyes and slender eyebrows which met in the middle. On her forehead she wore a streak of red paint.

At this moment I can picture Bugam Dasi, my mother, wearing a gold-embroidered sari of coloured silk and around her head a fillet of brocade, her bosom bare, her heavy tresses, black as the dark night of eternity, gathered in a knot behind her head, bracelets on her wrists and ankles and a gold ring in her nostril, with great, dark, languid, slanting eyes and brilliantly white teeth, dancing with slow, measured movements to the music of the sitar,* the

*A three-stringed instrument resembling a mandolin.

drum, the lute, the cymbal and the horn, a soft, monotonous music played by bare-bodied men in turbans, a music of mysterious significance, concentrating in itself all the secrets of wizardry, the legends, the passion and the sorrow of the men of India; and, as she performs her rhythmic evolutions, her voluptuous gestures, the consecrated movements of the temple dance, Bugam Dasi unfolds like the petals of a flower. A tremor passes across her shoulders and arms, she bends forward and again shrinks back. Each movement has its own precise meaning and speaks a language that is not of words. What an effect must all this have had upon my father! Above all, the voluptuous significance of the spectacle was intensified by the acrid, peppery smell of her sweat mingling with the perfume of champac and sandalwood oil, perfumes redolent of the essences of exotic trees and arousing sensations that slumbered hitherto in the depths of the consciousness. I imagine these perfumes as resembling the smell of the drug box, of the drugs which used to be kept in the nursery and which, we were told, came from India—unknown oils from a land of mystery, of ancient civilisation. I feel sure that the medicines I used to take had that smell.

All these things revived distant, dead memories in my father's mind. He fell in love with Bugam Dasi, so deeply in love that he embraced the dancing-girl's religion, the lingam cult.

After some time the girl became pregnant and was discharged from the service of the temple. Shortly after I was born my uncle returned to Benares from one of his trips. Apparently, in the matter of women as in all others, his reactions were identical with my father's. He fell passionately in love with my mother and in the end he satisfied his desire, which, because of his physical and mental resemblance to my father, was not difficult for him to do. As soon as she learned the truth my mother said that she would never again have anything to do with either of them unless they agreed to undergo 'trial by cobra'. In that case she would belong to whichever of the two came through alive.

The 'trial' consisted of the following. My father and my uncle would be enclosed together in a dark room like a dungeon in which a cobra had been let loose. The first of them to be bitten by the serpent would, naturally, cry out. Immediately a snake charmer would open the door of the room and bring the other out into safety. Bugam Dasi would belong to the survivor.

Before the two were shut up in the dark room my father asked Bugam Dasi if she would perform the sacred temple dance before him once more. She agreed to do so and, by torchlight, to the music of the snake charmer's pipe, she danced, with her significant, measured, gliding movements, bending and twisting like a cobra. Then my father and uncle were shut up in the room with the serpent. Instead of a shriek of horror what the listeners heard was a groan blended with a wild, gooseflesh-raising peal of laughter. When the door was opened my uncle walked out of the dark room. His face was ravaged and old, and his hair—the terror aroused by the sound of the cobra's body as it slid across the floor, by its furious hissing, by its glittering eyes, by the thought of its poisonous fangs and of its loathsome body shaped like a long neck terminating in a spoon-shaped protuberance and a tiny head, the horror of all this had changed my uncle, by the time he walked out of the room, into a white-haired old man.

In accordance with the terms of the contract Bugam Dasi belonged henceforth to my uncle. The frightful thing was that it was not certain that the survivor actually was my uncle. The 'trial' had deranged his mind and he had completely lost his memory. He did not recognise the infant and it was this that made them decide he must be my uncle. May it not be that this story has some strange bearing upon my personal history and that that gooseflesh-raising peal of laughter and the horror of the 'trial by cobra' have left their imprint upon me and are somehow pertinent to my destiny?

From this time on I was nothing more than an intruder, an extra mouth to feed. In the end my uncle (or my father, whichever it was), accompanied by Bugam Dasi, returned to the city of Rey on business. They brought me with them and left me with his sister, my aunt.

My nurse told me that my mother, when saying goodbye, handed my aunt a bottle of wine to keep for me. It was a deep red wine, and it contained a portion of the venom of the cobra, the Indian serpent. What more suitable keepsake could such a woman as Bugam Dasi have found to leave to her child? Deep red wine, an elixir of death which would bestow everlasting peace. Perhaps she also had pressed out her life like a cluster of grapes and was now giving me the wine which it had yielded, that same venom which had killed my father. I understand now how precious was the gift she gave me.

Is my mother still alive? Perhaps at this moment as I write she is bending and twisting like a serpent, as though it were she whom the cobra had bitten, dancing by torchlight in an open space in some far-off city of India, while women and children and intent, bare-bodied men stand around her and my father (or my uncle), white-haired and bent, sits somewhere on the edge of the circle watching her and remembers the dungeon and the hissing of the angry cobra as it glided forward, its head raised high, its neck swelling like a scoop and the spectacle-shaped lines on the back of its hood steadily expanding and deepening in colour.

At all events I was a little baby when I was entrusted to the care of my nurse. Nanny also suckled my aunt's daughter, the bitch my wife. I grew up in the family of my aunt, the tall woman with the grey hair around her temples, in the same house as the bitch, her daughter.

Ever since I can remember I looked upon my aunt as a mother and loved her deeply. I loved her so deeply that later on I married her daughter, my foster sister, simply because she looked like her.

Or rather, I was forced to marry her. She gave herself to me only once. I shall never forget it. It happened by the bedside of her dead mother. Late at night, after everyone had gone to bed, I got up in my nightshirt and drawers and went into the dead woman's room to say goodbye to her for the last time. Two camphor candles were burning at her head. A Koran had been laid on her stomach to prevent the Devil from entering her body. I drew back the sheet which covered her and saw my aunt again, with her dignified, pleasant face, from which, it seemed, all traces of earthly concerns had been effaced. She wore an expression before which I involuntarily bowed my head and at the same time I felt that death was a normal, natural thing. The corners of her lips were fixed in a faintly ironical smile. I was about to kiss her hand and go out when, turning my head, I saw with a start that the bitch who is now my wife had come into the room. There in the presence of her dead mother she pressed herself hard against me, held me close and kissed me long and passionately on the lips. I could have sunk into the ground with shame, but I had not the strength of mind to do what I should have done. The dead woman, her teeth visible, looked as though she was mocking us—I had the impression that her expression had changed from the quiet smile she had been wearing before. Mechanically I held the girl in my arms and returned her kiss, when suddenly the curtain draped across the doorway leading to the next room was drawn aside and my aunt's husband, the bitch's father, came into the room. He was a bent old man, and he was wearing a scarf wrapped around his neck.

He burst into a hollow, grating, gooseflesh-raising peal of laughter, of a quality to make the hairs on one's body stand on end. His shoulders were shaking. And yet he did not look in our direction. I could have sunk into the ground with shame. If I had had the strength I should have slapped the dead face which was gazing mockingly at us. I was overcome with shame and fled blindly from the room. And I had the bitch to thank! The chances are that she had arranged the whole thing in advance so as to put me into a position where I should be forced to marry her.

And in fact, foster brother and sister though we were, I was obliged to marry her to save her reputation. She was not a virgin, but I was unaware of the fact, and indeed was in no position to know of it; I only learnt it later from people's gossip. When we were alone together in the bridal chamber on the first night she refused to undress, despite all my begging and praying, and would only say, 'It's the wrong time of the month'. She would not let me come near her but put out the light and lay down to sleep on the other side of the room from me. She was trembling like a willow tree. Anyone might have thought she had been shut up in a dungeon with a dragon. I shall probably not be believed—and indeed the thing passes belief—when I say that she did not once allow me to kiss her on the lips.

The next night also I slept on the floor as I had done the night before, and similarly on the night that followed. I could not work up the courage to do anything else. And so a considerable period went by, during which I slept on the floor on the other side of the room from my wife. Who would believe it? For two months—no, for two months and four days—I slept apart from her on the floor and could not work up the courage to come near her.

She had prepared her virginity token beforehand. I don't know—perhaps she had sprinkled the cloth with the blood of a partridge or perhaps it was a cloth she had kept from the first night of her gallantries in order to make a bigger fool of me. At the time everyone was congratulating me. They were winking at one another and I suppose they were saying to one another, 'The lad took the fortress by storm last night', while I put the best face on it that I could and pretended I noticed nothing. They were laughing at me, at my blindness. I made a resolution to write the whole story down some day.

I found out later that she had lovers right and left. It may be that the reason she hated me was that a preacher, by the process of reciting a few words in Arabic over us, had placed her under my authority; perhaps she simply wanted to be free. Finally, one night I made up my mind to share her bed by force, and I carried out my resolve. After a tussle she got out of the bed and left me and the only satisfaction I had was that I was able to curl up and sleep the rest of the night in her bed, which was impregnated with the warmth and the odour of her body. The only time I enjoyed peaceful sleep was that night. After that she slept in a different room from me.

When I came back to the house after dark she would still be out. Or rather, I would not know whether she had returned home or not and I did not care to know, since solitude and death were my destiny. I desired at all costs to establish contact with her lovers—this is another thing that will seem incredible—and sought out everyone who I heard had caught her fancy. I put up with every sort of humiliation in order to strike up an acquaintance with them. I toadied to them, urged them to visit my wife, even brought them to the house. And what people she chose! A tripe-pedlar, an interpreter of the Law, a cooked-meat vendor, the police superintendent, a shady mufti, a philosopher—their names and titles varied, but none of them was fit to be anything better than assistant to the man who sells boiled sheep's heads. And she preferred all of them to me. No one would believe me if I were to describe the abject self-abasement with which I cringed and grovelled to her and them. The reason why I behaved like this was that I was afraid my wife might leave me. I wanted my wife's lovers to teach me deportment, manners, the technique of seduction! However, as a pimp I was not a success, and the fools all laughed in my face. After all, how ever could I have learnt manners and deportment from the rabble? I know now that she loved them precisely because they were shameless, stupid and rotten. Her love was inseparable from filth and death. Did I really want to sleep with her? Was it her looks that had made me fall in love with her, or was it her aversion to me or her general behaviour or the deep affection I had felt for her mother since my early childhood, or was it all of these things combined? I simply do not know. One thing I do know: my wife, the bitch, the sorceress, had poured into my soul some poison which not only made me want her but made every single atom in my body desire the atoms of hers and shriek aloud its desire. I yearned to be with her on some lost island where there would be nobody but us two. I wished that an earthquake, a great storm or a thunderbolt from the sky might blast all the rabble-humanity that was there breathing, bustling and enjoying life on the far side of the wall of my room and that only she and I might remain.

But even then would she not have preferred any other living creature—an Indian serpent, a dragon—to me? I longed to spend one night with her and to die together with her, locked in her arms. I felt that this would be the sublime culmination of my existence.

While I wasted away in agony the bitch for her part seemed to derive an exquisite pleasure from torturing me. In the end I abandoned all the activities and interests that I had and remained confined to my room like a living corpse. No one knew the secret which existed between us. Even my old nurse, who was a witness of my slow death, used to reproach me—on account of the bitch! Behind my back, around me, I heard people whispering, 'How can that poor woman put up with that crazy husband of hers?' And they were right, for my abasement had gone beyond all conceivable limits.

I wasted away from day to day. When I looked at myself in the mirror my cheeks were crimson like the meat that hangs outside butchers' shops. My body was glowing with heat and the expression of my eyes was languid and depressed.

I was pleased with the change in my appearance. I had seen the dust of death sprinkled over my eyes, I had seen that I must go.

At last they sent word to the doctor, the rabble doctor, the family doctor who, in his own words, had 'brought us all up'. He came into the room in an embroidered turban and with a beard three handsbreadths long. It was his boast that he had in his time given my grandfather drugs to restore his virility, administered grey powders to me and forced cassia down the throat of my aunt. He sat down by my bedside and, after feeling my pulse and inspecting my tongue, gave his professional advice: I was to go onto a diet of ass's milk and barley water and to have my room fumigated twice a day with mastic and arsenic. He also gave my nurse a number of lengthy prescriptions consisting of herbal extracts and weird and wonderful oils—hyssop, olive oil, extract of liquorice, camphor, maidenhair, camomile oil, oil of bay, linseed, fir-tree nuts and such-like trash.

My condition grew worse. Only my old grey-haired nurse, who was *her* nurse also, attended me, bringing me my medicine or sitting beside my bed, dabbing cold water on my forehead. She would talk about the time when the bitch and I were children. For example, she told me how my wife from early childhood had a habit of biting the nails of her left hand and would sometimes gnaw them to the quick. Sometimes she would tell me stories and then I would feel that my life had reversed its course and I had become a child again, for the stories were intimately associated with my memories of those days. I remember quite plainly that when I was very little and my wife and I used to sleep together in the one cradle, a big double cradle, my nurse used to tell the same stories. Some things in these stories which then used to strike me as far-fetched now seem perfectly natural and credible to me.

My morbid condition had created within me a new world, a strange indistinct world of shapes and colours and desires of which a healthy person could have no conception. In these circumstances the crowding incidents of my nurse's tales struck an echo which filled me with indescribable delight and agitation. I felt that I had become a child again. At this very moment as I write I experience those sensations. They belong, all of them, to the present. They are not an element of the past.

It would seem that the behaviour, thoughts, aspirations and customs of the men of past ages, as transmitted to later generations by the medium of such stories, are among the essential components of human life. For thousands of years people have been saying the same words, performing the same sexual act, vexing themselves with the same childish worries. Is not life from beginning to end a ludicrous story, an improbable, stupid yarn? Am I not now writing my own personal piece of fiction? A story is only an outlet for frustrated aspirations, for aspirations which the storyteller conceives in accordance with a limited stock of spiritual resources inherited from previous generations.

If only I could have slept peacefully as I did in the days when I was an innocent child! Then I slept tranquil and easy. Now when I awoke my cheeks were crimson like the meat which hangs in front of butchers' shops, my body was burning hot and I coughed—how deep and horrible my cough was! It was impossible to imagine from what remote cavity of my body it proceeded. It resembled the coughing of the horses that bring the sheep carcases each morning to the butcher's shop opposite my window.

I remember well, the room was quite dark. I lay still for several minutes in a state of semiconsciousness. I used to talk to myself before I fell asleep. On this occasion I was convinced that I had become a child again and that I was lying in the cradle. I sensed that there was someone near me. Everyone in the house had long been in bed. It was the hour just before dawn, the time when, as sick people know, one's being seems to transcend the boundaries of the world.

My heart was beating hard but I experienced no fear. My eyes were open but I could see no one, for the darkness was intense. Several minutes passed. An idea, a sick man's idea, came into my mind. I said to myself, 'Perhaps it is she!' At the same moment I felt a cool hand laid on my burning forehead.

I shuddered. Two or three times I wondered if it was the hand of Ezraïl.* Then I fell asleep. When I awoke in the morning my nurse said to me, 'My daughter'—she meant the bitch, my wife—'came to your bedside and took your head in her lap and rocked you like a baby.' Apparently a maternal feeling had suddenly awakened in her. I wish I could have died at that moment. Perhaps the child she was pregnant with had died. Had she had her baby? I did not know.

Lying in this room of mine, which was steadily shrinking and growing dark like the grave, I had watched the door throughout my waking hours in the hope that my wife would come to me. But she never did. Was not she to blame for the condition I was in? For three years, or, rather for two years and four months—although, what do days and months matter? To me they mean nothing; time has no meaning for one who is lying in the grave—this room has been the tomb of my existence, the tomb of my mind. All the bustle, noise and pretence that filled the lives of other

*The Angel of Death.

people, the rabble-people who, body and soul, are turned out of the one mould, had become foreign and meaningless to me. Ever since I had been confined to my bed I had been living in a strange unimaginable world in which I had no need of the world of the rabble. It was a world which existed within me, a world of unknowns, and I felt an inner compulsion to probe and investigate every nook and cranny of it.

During the night, at the time when my being hovered on the boundary of the two worlds, immediately before I sank into a deep, blank sleep, I used to dream. In the course of a single second I lived a life which was entirely distinct from my waking life. I breathed a different atmosphere in some far-off region. It was probably that I wished to escape from myself and to change my destiny. When I shut my eyes my own real world was revealed to me. The images that I saw had an independent life of their own. They faded and reappeared at will and my volition appeared to exercise no control over them. This point, however, is not certain. The scenes which passed before my eyes were no ordinary dream, for I was not yet asleep. In silence and tranquillity I distinguished the various images and compared them with one another. It seemed to me that until now I had not known myself and that the world as I had conceived it hitherto had lost all significance and validity and had been replaced by the darkness of night. For I had not been taught to gaze at and to love the night.

I am not sure whether or not I had control of my arms at such times. I felt however that if once I were to leave my hand to its own resources it would begin to function spontaneously, impelled by some mysterious motive force of its own, without my being able to influence or master its movements, and that if I had not constantly kept careful watch of my body and automatically controlled it, it would have been capable of doing things which I did not in the least expect.

A sensation which had long been familiar to me was this, that I was slowly decomposing while I yet lived. My heart had always been at odds not only with my body but with my mind, and there was absolutely no compatibility between them. I had always been in a state of decomposition and gradual disintegration. At times I conceived thoughts which I myself felt to be inconceivable. At other times I experienced a feeling of pity for which my reason reproved me. Frequently when talking or engaged in business with someone I would begin to argue on this or that subject while all my feelings were somewhere else and I was thinking of something quite different and at the same time reproaching myself. I was a crumbling, decomposing mass. It seemed to me that this was what I had always been and always would be, a strange compound of incompatible elements. . . .

A thought which I found intolerably painful was this: whereas I felt that I was far removed from all the people whom I saw and among whom I lived, yet at the same time

I was related to them by an external similarity which was both remote and close. My surprise at the fact was diminished by the knowledge that my physical needs were the same as theirs. The point of resemblance which tortured me more than any other was the fact that the rabble-men were attracted as I was to the bitch, my wife, she feeling a stronger appetite for them than for me. I am certain that there was something lacking in the make-up of one of us.

I call her 'the bitch' because no other name would suit her so well. I do not like to say simply 'my wife', because the man-wife relationship did not exist between us and I should be lying to myself if I called her so. From the beginning of time I have called her 'the bitch', and the word has had a curious charm for me. If I married her it was because she made the first advances. She did so by design and fraud. No, she had no kindness for me. How could she ever have felt kindness for anyone? A sensual creature who required one man to satisfy her lust, another to play the gallant and another to satisfy her need to inflict pain. Not that I think she restricted herself to this trinity, but at any rate I was the one she selected to torture. To tell the truth she could not have chosen a better subject. For my part I married her because she looked like her mother and because she had a faint, remote resemblance to me. And by this time not merely did I love her but every atom in my body desired her. And, more than any other part of me, my loins—for I refuse to hide real feelings behind a fanciful veil of 'love', 'fondness' and such-like theological terms: I have no taste for literary *huz-varesh*.* I felt as though both of us had pulsating in our loins a kind of radiation or aureole like those which one sees depicted around the heads of the prophets and that my sickly, diseased aureole was seeking hers and striving with all its might towards it.

When my condition improved I made up my mind to go away, to go somewhere where people would never find me again, like a dog with distemper who knows that he is going to die or like the birds that hide themselves when the time to die has come. Early one morning I rose, dressed, took a couple of cakes that were lying on the top shelf and, without attracting anyone's attention, fled from the house. I was running away from my own misery. I walked aimlessly along the streets, I wandered without set purpose among the rabble-men as they hurried by, an expression of greed on their faces, in pursuit of money and sexual satisfaction. I had no need to see them since anyone of them was a sample of the lot. Each and every one of them consisted only of a mouth and a wad of guts hanging from it, the whole terminating in a set of genitals.

I felt that I had suddenly become lighter and more agile. My leg muscles were functioning with a suppleness and speed which until then I could not have imagined to

*A convention of Pahlavi writing by which the scribe substituted an Aramaic word for a Persian one.

be possible. I felt that I had escaped from all the fetters of existence and that this was my natural mode of movement. In my childhood, whenever I had slipped off the burden of trouble and responsibility, I had walked like this.

The sun was already high in the sky and the heat was intense. I found myself walking along deserted streets lined with ash-grey houses of strange, geometrical shapes—cubes, prisms, cones—with low, dark windows. One felt that these windows were never opened, that the houses were untenanted, temporary structures and that no living creature could ever have dwelt in them.

The sun, like a golden knife, was steadily paring away the edge of the shade beside the walls. The streets were enclosed between old, whitewashed walls. Everywhere were peace and stillness, as though all the elements were obeying the sacred law of calm and silence imposed by the blazing heat. It seemed as though mystery was everywhere and my lungs hardly dared to inhale the air.

All at once I became aware that I was outside the gate of the city. The sun, sucking with a thousand mouths, was drawing the sweat of my body. The desert plants looked, under the great, blazing sun, like so many patches of turmeric. The sun was like a feverish eye. It poured its burning rays from the depths of the sky over the silent; lifeless landscape. The ground and the plants gave off a peculiar smell which brought back certain moments of my childhood. Not only did it evoke actions and words from that period of my life, but for a moment I felt as though that time had returned and these things had happened only the day before. I experienced a kind of agreeable giddiness. It seemed to me that I had been born again in an infinitely remote world. This sensation had an intoxicating quality and, like an old sweet wine, affected every vein and nerve in my body. I recognised the thornbushes, the stones, the tree stumps and the low shrubs of wild thyme. I recognised the familiar smell of the grass. Long past days of my life came back to me, but all these memories, in some strange fashion, were curiously remote from me and led an independent life of their own, in such a way that I was no more than a passive and distant witness and felt that my heart was empty now and that the perfume of the plants had lost the magic which it had had in those days. The cypress trees were more thinly spaced, the hills had grown more arid. The person that I had been then existed no longer. If I had been able to conjure him up and to speak to him he would not have listened to me and, if he had, would not have understood what I said. He was like someone whom I had known once, but he was no part of me.

The world seemed to me like a forlorn, empty house and my heart was filled with trepidation, as though I were now obliged to go barefoot and explore every room in that house: I would pass through room after room, but when I reached the last of all and found myself face to face with 'the bitch' the doors behind me would shut of their own accord and only the quivering, blurred shadows of the walls would stand guard, like black slaves, around me.

I had nearly reached the river Suran when I found myself at the foot of a barren, stony hill. Its lean, hard contours put me in mind of my nurse; there was an indefinable resemblance between them. I skirted the hill and came upon a small, green enclosure surrounded on every side by hills. The level ground was covered with vines of morning glory, and on one of the hills stood a lofty castle built of massive bricks.

I suddenly realised that I was tired. I walked up to the Suran and sat down on the fine sand on its bank in the shade of an old cypress tree. It was a peaceful, lonely spot. I felt that no one until then had ever set foot there. All at once I saw a little girl appear from behind the cypress trees and set off in the direction of the castle. She was wearing a black dress of very fine, light material, apparently silk. She was biting the nail of one of the fingers of her left hand, and she glided by with an unconstrained, carefree air. I had the feeling that I had seen her before and knew who she was but could not be sure. Suddenly she vanished. Where she had gone, the distance between us and the glare of the sun prevented me from making out.

I remained petrified, unable to make the slightest movement. I was quite sure that I had seen her with my own two eyes walk past and then disappear. Was she a real being or an illusion? Had I seen her in a dream or waking? All my attempts to call her face to mind were vain. I experienced a peculiar tremor down my spine. It occurred to me that this was the hour of the day when the shadows of the castle upon the hill returned to life, and that this little girl was one of the old-time inhabitants of the ancient city of Rey.

The landscape before my eyes all at once struck me as familiar. I remembered that once in my childhood on the thirteenth day of Nouruz I had come here with my mother-in-law and 'the bitch'. That day we ran after each other and played for hours on the far side of these same cypress trees. Then we were joined by another band of children—who they were, I cannot quite remember. We played hide-and-seek together. Once when I was running after the bitch on the bank of the Suran her foot slipped and she fell into the water. The others pulled her out and took her behind the cypress tree to change her clothes. I followed them. They hung up a woman's veil as a screen in front of her but I furtively peeped from behind a tree and saw her whole body. She was smiling and biting the nail of the index-finger of her left hand. Then they wrapped her up in a white cloak and spread out her fine-textured black silk dress to dry in the sun.

I stretched myself out at full length on the fine sand at the foot of the old cypress tree. The babbling of the water reached my ears like the staccato, unintelligible syllables murmured by a man who is dreaming. I automatically thrust my hands into the warm, moist sand. I squeezed the warm, moist sand in my fists. It felt like the firm flesh of a girl who has fallen into the water and who has changed her clothes.

I do not know how long I spent thus. When I stood up I began automatically to walk. The whole countryside was silent and peaceful. I walked on, completely unaware of my surroundings. Some force beyond my control compelled me to keep moving. All of my attention was concentrated on my feet. I did not walk in the normal fashion but glided along as the girl in black had done.

When I came to myself I found that I was back in the city and standing before my father-in-law's house. I do not know why the route I had followed had chanced to lead me to my father-in-law's house. His little son, my brother-in-law, was sitting on the stone bench outside. He and his sister were like two halves of the one apple. He had slanting Turkoman eyes, prominent cheekbones, a complexion the colour of ripe wheat, sensual nostrils and a strong, thin face. As he sat there he was holding the index finger of his left hand to his lips. I automatically went up to him, put my hand into my pocket, took out the two cakes, gave them to him and said, 'These are for you from Mummy'—he used to call my wife 'Mummy' for want of a real mother. He took the cakes with some hesitation and looked at them with an expression of surprise in his Turkoman eyes. I sat down beside him on the bench. I set him on my lap and pressed him to me. His body was warm and the calves of his legs reminded me of my wife's. He had the same unconstrained manner as she. His lips were like his father's, but what in the father aroused my aversion I found charming and attractive in the boy. They were half-open, as though they had only just broken away from a long, passionate kiss. I kissed him on his half-open mouth, which was so much like my wife's. His lips tasted like the stub end of a cucumber: they were acrid and bitter. The bitch's lips, I thought, must have the same taste.

At that moment I caught sight of his father, the bent old man with the scarf around his neck, coming out of the doorway. He passed by without looking in my direction. He was laughing convulsively. It was a horrible laugh, of a quality to make the hairs on one's body stand on end, and he laughed so that his shoulders shook. I could have sunk into the ground with shame. It was shortly before sunset. I stood up, wishing that I could somehow escape from myself. Mechanically, I took the direction that led to my own house. I saw nothing and nobody in the street. It seemed to me that I was walking through a strange, unknown city. Around me were weird isolated houses of geometrical shapes, with forlorn, black windows. One felt that no creature with the breath of life in it could ever have dwelt in them. Their white walls gave off a sickly radiance. A strange, an unbelievable thing was this: whenever I stopped, my shadow fell long and black on the wall in the moonlight, but it had no head. I had heard people say that if anyone casts a headless shadow on a wall that person would die before the year was out.

Overcome with fear, I went into my house and shut myself up in my room. At the same moment I began to bleed from the nose. After losing a great quantity of blood I collapsed upon my bed. My nurse came in to see to me.

Before I went to sleep I looked at myself in the mirror. My face was ravaged, lifeless and indistinct, so indistinct that I did not recognise myself. I got into bed, pulled the quilt over my head, huddled myself up and, with eyes closed, pursued the course of my thoughts. I was conscious of the strands which had been woven by a dark, gloomy, fearful and delightful destiny; I moved in the regions where life and death fuse together and perverse images come into being and ancient, extinct desires, vague, strangled desires, again come to life and cry aloud for vengeance. For that space of time I was severed from nature and the phenomenal world and was prepared to accept effacement and dissolution in the everlasting flux. I murmured again and again, 'Death, death . . . where are you?' The thought of death soothed me and I fell asleep.

In my sleep I dreamed. I was in the Mohammadiyye square. A tall gallows tree had been erected there and the body of the old odds-and-ends man whom I used to see from my window was hanging from its arm. At its foot were several drunken policemen drinking wine. My mother-in-law, in a state of great excitement, with the expression which I see on my wife's face when she is badly upset—bloodless lips, staring, wild eyes—was dragging me by the arm through the crowd, gesticulating to the red-clad hangman and shouting, 'String this one up too!' I awoke in terror. I was glowing like a furnace, my body was streaming with sweat and my cheeks were burning. In order to get the nightmare out of my mind I rose, drank some water and dabbed my head and face. I went back to bed but could not fall asleep.

Lying there in the transparent darkness I gazed steadily at the water jug that stood on the topmost shelf. I had an irrational fear that it was going to fall and decided that so long as it stood there I should be unable to fall asleep. I got up, intending to put the jug in a safe place, but by some obscure impulsion that had nothing to do with me my hand deliberately nudged it so that it fell and was smashed to pieces. I was able to close my eyes at last but I had the feeling that my nurse had come into the room and was looking at me. I clenched my fists under the quilt but in fact nothing out of the ordinary happened. In a state of semiconsciousness I heard the street door open and recognised the sound of my nurse's steps as, shuffling her slippers along the ground, she went to buy bread and cheese for breakfast. Then came the far-off cry of a street vendor, 'Mulberries for your bile!' No, life, wearisome as ever, had begun again. The light was growing brighter. When I opened my eyes a patch of sunlight reflected from the surface of the tank outside my window was flickering on the ceiling.

I felt that the dream of the night had receded and faded like one seen years before during my childhood. My nurse brought me in my breakfast. Her face was like a reflection in a distorting mirror, it was so lean and drawn and seemed to have acquired such an unnatural, comical shape. One might have thought that it had been stretched out by some heavy weight fastened to the chin.

Although Nanny knew that nargileh smoke was bad for me, nonetheless she used to bring a nargileh with her when she came into my room. The fact is that she never felt quite herself until she had had a smoke. With all her chit-chat about her family affairs, about her son and her daughter-in-law, she had made me a participant in her intimate life. Stupid as it may seem, I would sometimes find myself ruminating idly about the doings of the members of my nurse's family. For some reason all activity, all happiness on the part of other people, made me feel like vomiting. I was aware that my own life was finished and was slowly and painfully guttering out. What earthly reason had I to concern myself with the lives of the fools, the rabble-people who were fit and healthy, ate well, slept well, and copulated well and who had never experienced a particle of my sufferings or felt the wings of death every minute brushing against their faces?

Nanny treated me like a child. She tried to pry into every cranny of my mind. I was still shy of my wife. Whenever she came into the room I would cover up the phlegm which I had spat into the basin; I would comb my hair and beard and set my nightcap straight on my head. But I had no trace of shyness with nurse. How had that woman, who was so utterly different from me, managed to occupy so large a zone of my life? I remember how in the winter time they used to set up a *korsi** in this same room above the cistern. My nurse and I and the bitch would go to sleep around the *korsi*. When I opened my eyes in the transparent darkness the design on the embroidered curtain that hung in the doorway opposite me would come to life. What a strange, disquieting curtain it was! On it was depicted a bent old man like an Indian fakir with a turban on his head. He was sitting under a cypress tree, holding a musical instrument that resembled a *sitar*. Before him stood a beautiful young girl, such a girl as I imagined Bugam Dasi, the Indian temple dancer, to have been. Her hands were bound and it seemed that she was obliged to dance before the old man. I used to think to myself that perhaps this old man had been shut up in a dungeon with a cobra and that it was this experience that had bent him double and turned his hair and beard white. It was a gold-embroidered Indian curtain such as my father (or my uncle) might have sent from abroad. Whenever I happened to gaze for a long time at the design upon it

*A stool under which is placed a lighted brazier and over which blankets are spread. People recline with the lower part of their bodies under the blankets.

I would become frightened and, half-asleep as I was, would wake up my nurse. She, with her bad breath and her coarse black hair against my face, would hold me close to her.

When I awoke in the morning she looked exactly the same to me as she did on those days, except that the lines of her face were deeper and harder.

I often used to recall the days of my childhood in order to forget the present, in order to escape from myself. I tried to feel as I did in the days before I fell ill. Then I would have the sensation that I was still a child and that inside me there was a second self which felt sorry for this child who was about to die. In my moments of crisis one glimpse of my nurse's calm, pallid face with its deepset, dim, unmoving eyes, thin nostrils and broad, bony forehead, was enough to revive in me the sensations of my childhood. Perhaps she emitted some mysterious radiation which created this peace of mind in me.

On her forehead there was a fleshy birthmark with hairs sprouting from it. I do not remember having noticed it before today. Previously when I looked at her face I did not scrutinise it so closely.

Although Nanny had changed outwardly her ideas remained what they had always been. The only difference was that she evinced a greater fondness for life and seemed afraid of death, in which she reminded me of the flies which take refuge indoors at the beginning of the autumn. I on the other hand changed with every day and every minute.

It seemed to me that the passage of time had become thousands of times more rapid in my case than in that of other people and that the alterations I daily observed in myself should normally have been the work of years, whereas the satisfaction I should have derived from life tended, on the contrary, towards zero and perhaps even sank below zero. There are people whose death agonies begin at the age of twenty, while others die only at the very end, calmly and peacefully, like a lamp in which all the oil has been consumed.

When my nurse brought me my dinner at midday I upset the soup bowl and began to shriek at the top of my voice. Everyone in the house came running to my room and gathered at the door. The bitch came along with the rest but she soon went away again. I had a look at her belly. It was big and swollen. No, she had not had the baby yet. Someone went to fetch the doctor. I was delighted at the thought that at any rate I had given the fools trouble.

The doctor came, with his beard three handsbreadths long, and prescribed opium for me. What a marvellous remedy for the pains of my existence! Whenever I smoked opium my ideas aquired grandeur, subtlety, magic and sublimity and I moved in another sphere beyond boundaries of the ordinary world. My thoughts were freed from the weight of material reality and soared towards an empyrean of tranquillity and silence. I felt as though I was borne on the wings of a golden bat and ranged through a radiant, empty world with no obstacle to block my progress. So profound and delicious was the sensation I experienced that the delight it gave me was stronger than death itself.

When I stood up from beside my brazier I went over to the window facing onto the courtyard of our house. My nurse was sitting in the sun cleaning some vegetables. I heard her say to her daughter-in-law, 'We all feel very sorry for him. I only wish God would put him out of his misery.' So the doctor, apparently, had told them I was not going to get better.

It did not surprise me at all. What fools all these people were! When she brought me my medicine an hour later her eyes were red and swollen with weeping. She forced a smile when she saw me. They used to play-act in front of me, they all used to play-act in front of me, and how clumsily they did it! Did they suppose I did not know, myself? But why was this woman of all people so fond of me? Why did she feel that she had a share in my sufferings? All that had happened was that someone had come to her one day and given her money, and she had thrust her wrinkled black nipples, like little buckets, between my lips—and I wish that the canker had eaten them away! Whenever I saw them now I felt like vomiting to think that at that time I had greedily sucked out their life-giving juice while the warmth of our two bodies blended together. She had handled me all over when I was little and it was for this reason that she still treated me with that peculiar boldness that you find only in widows.

Just because at one time she used to hold me over the latrine she still looked on me as a child. Who knows? Perhaps she had used me as women use their adoptive sisters. . . .

Even now she missed nothing whenever she helped me to do the things which I could not do on my own. If the bitch my wife had shown any interest in me I should never have let Nanny come near me in her presence, because I felt that my wife had a wider range of ideas and a keener aesthetic sense than my nurse had. Or perhaps this bashfulness of mine was merely the result of my obsession.

At any rate I was not shy of my nurse, and she was the only one who looked after me. I suppose she thought it was all a matter of destiny and that it was her star that had saddled her with this responsibility. In any case she made the most of my illness and confided all her family troubles and joys to me, kept me posted on current quarrels and feuds and in general revealed all the simplicity, the cunning and the avarice which went into her make-up. She told me what a trial her daughter-in-law was to her and spoke with such feeling on the subject that one would have thought that the younger woman was a rival wife who had stolen a portion of her son's love for her. Obviously the daughter-in-law is good-looking. I saw her once in the courtyard from my window. She had grey eyes, fair hair and a small, straight nose.

Sometimes my nurse would talk about the miracles performed by the prophets. Her purpose in so doing was to entertain me but the only effect was to make me envy her the pettiness and stupidity of her ideas. Sometimes she retailed pieces of gossip. For example, she told me a few days ago that her daughter (meaning the bitch) had made a set of clothes for the baby—her baby. After which she began to console me in a way that suggested she knew the truth. Sometimes she would fetch me homemade remedies from the neighbours or she would consult magicians and fortune-tellers about my case. On the last Wednesday of the year she went to see one of her fortune-tellers and came back with a bowl of onions, rice and rancid oil. She told me she had begged this rubbish from the fortune-teller in the hope that it would help me to get better.* On the following days she gave it to me in small portions in my food without my knowledge. She also made me swallow at regular intervals the various concoctions prescribed by the doctor: hyssop, extract of liquorice, camphor, maidenhair, camomile, oil of bay, linseed, fir-tree nuts, starch, grey powders, and heaven knows how many more varieties of trash.

A few days ago she brought me a prayer book with half-an-inch of dust on it. I had no use, not only for prayer books, but for any sort of literature that expressed the notions of the rabble. What need had I of their nonsense and

*It is the custom of the last Wednesday before Nouruz for people to disguise themselves and go begging. The alms received on this occasion are believed to bring good luck.

lies? Was not I myself the result of a long succession of past generations which had bequeathed their experience to me? Did not the past exist within me? As for mosques, the muezzin's call to prayer, the ceremonial washing of the body and rinsing of the mouth, not to mention the pious practice of bobbing up and down in honour of a high and mighty Being, the omnipotent Lord of all things, with whom it was impossible to have a chat except in the Arabic language—these things left me completely cold.

Earlier, in the days before I fell ill, I had been to the mosque a number of times, always more or less unwillingly. On these occasions I had tried to enter into a community of feeling with the people around me. But my eye would rest on the shining, patterned tiles on the wall and I would be transported into a delightful dream world. Thereby I unconsciously provided myself with a way of escape. During the prayers I would shut my eyes and cover my face with my hand and in this artificial night of my own making I would recite the prayers like the meaningless sounds uttered by someone who is dreaming. The words were not spoken from the heart. I found it pleasanter to talk to a friend or acquaintance than to God, the high and mighty One. God was too important a personage for me.

When I was lying in my warm, damp bed these questions did not interest me one jot and at such a time it did not matter to me whether God really existed or whether He was nothing but a personification of the mighty ones of this world, invented for the greater glory of spiritual values and the easier spoliation of the lower orders, the pattern of earthly things being transferred to the sky. All that I wanted to know was whether or not I was going to live through to the morning. In face of death I felt that religion, faith, belief were feeble, childish things of which the best that could be said was that they provided a kind of recreation for healthy, successful people. In face of the frightful reality of death and of my own desperate condition, all that had been inculcated into me on the subject of judgment day and rewards and penalties in a future life seemed an insipid fraud, and the prayers I had been taught were completely ineffective against the fear of death.

No, the fear of death would not let me go. People who have not known suffering themselves will not understand me when I say that my attachment to life had grown so strong that the least moment of ease compensated for long hours of palpitation and anguish.

I saw that pain and disease existed and at the same time that they were void of sense and meaning. Among the men of the rabble I had become a creature of a strange, unknown race, so much so that they had forgotten that I had once been part of their world. I had the dreadful sensation that I was not really alive or wholly dead. I was a living corpse, unrelated to the world of living people and at the same time deprived of the oblivion and peace of death.

It was night when I stood up from beside my opium brazier. I looked out of the window. A single black tree was visible beside the shuttered butcher's shop. The shadows had merged into one black mass. I felt as though everything in the world was hollow and provisional. The pitch-black sky reminded me of an old black tent in which the countless shining stars represented holes. As I watched I heard from somewhere the voice of a muezzin, although it was not the time for the call to prayer. It sounded like the cry of a woman—it could have been the bitch—in the pangs of childbirth. Mingled with the cry was the sound of a dog howling. I thought to myself, 'If it is true that everyone has his own star in the sky mine must be remote, dark and meaningless. Perhaps I have never had a star at all.'

Just then the voices of a band of drunken policemen rose loud from the street. As they marched by they were joking obscenely among themselves. Then they began to sing in chorus,

> *'Come, let us go and drink wine;*
> *Let us drink wine of the Kingdom of Rey.*
> *If we do not drink now, when should we drink?'*

In terror I shrank back from the window. Their voices resounded strangely through the night air, gradually growing fainter and fainter. No, they were not coming for me, they did not know. . . . Silence and darkness settled down upon the world again. I did not light my oil lamp. It was more pleasant to sit in the dark, that dense liquid which permeates everything and every place. I had grown accustomed to the dark. It was in the dark that my lost thoughts, my forgotten fears, the frightful, unbelievable ideas that had been lurking in some unknown recess of my brain, used to return to life, to move about and to grimace at me. In the corners of my room, behind the curtains, beside the door, were hosts of these ideas, of these formless, menacing figures.

There, beside the curtain, sat one fearful shape. It never stirred, it was neither gloomy nor cheerful. Every time I came back to my room it gazed steadily into my eyes. Its face was familiar to me. It seemed to me that I had seen that face at some time in my childhood. Yes, it was on the thirteenth day of Nouruz. I was playing hide-and-seek with some other children on the bank of the river Suran when I caught sight of that same face amid a crowd of other, ordinary faces set on top of funny, reassuring little bodies. It reminded me of the butcher opposite the window of my room. I felt that this shape had its place in my life and that I had seen it often before. Perhaps this shadow had been born along with me and moved within the restricted circuit of my existence. . . .

As soon as I stood up to light the lamp the shape faded and disappeared. I stood in front of the mirror and stared at my face. The reflection that I saw was unfamiliar to me. It was a weird, frightening image. My reflection had become stronger than my real self and I had become like an image in a mirror. I felt that I could not remain alone in the same room with my reflection. I was afraid that if I tried to run away he would come after me. We were like two cats face to face, preparing to do battle. But I knew that I could create my own complete darkness with the hollow of my palm and I raised my hand and covered my eyes. The sensation of horror as usual aroused in me a feeling of exquisite, intoxicating pleasure which made my head swim and my knees give way and filled me with nausea. Suddenly I realised that I was still standing. The circumstance struck me as odd, even inexplicable. How could it have come about that I was standing on my feet? It seemed to me that if I were to move one of my feet I should lose my balance. A kind of vertigo took possession of me. The earth and everything upon it had receded infinitely far from me. I wished vaguely for an earthquake or a thunderbolt from the sky which would make it possible for me to be born again in a world of light and peace.

When at last I went back to bed, I said to myself, 'Death . . . death. . . .' My lips were closed, yet I was afraid of my voice. I had quite lost my previous boldness. I had become like the flies which crowd indoors at the beginning of the autumn, thin, half-dead flies which are afraid at first of the buzzing of their own wings and cling to some one point of the wall until they realise that they are alive; then they fling themselves recklessly against door and walls until they fall dead around the floor.

As my eyes closed a dim, indistinct world began to take shape around me. It was a world of which I was the sole creator and which was in perfect harmony with my vision of reality. At all events it was far more real and natural to me than my waking world and presented no obstacle, no barrier, to my ideas. In it time and place lost their validity. My repressed lusts, my secret needs, which had begotten this dream, gave rise to shapes and to happenings which were beyond belief but which seemed natural to me. For a few moments after waking up I had no sense of time or place and doubted whether I really existed. It would seem that I myself created all my dreams and had long known the correct interpretation of them.

A great part of the night had passed by the time I fell asleep. All at once I found myself wandering free and unconstrained through an unknown town, along streets lined with weird houses of geometrical shapes—prisms, cones, cubes—with low, dark windows and doors and walls overgrown with vines of morning glory. All the inhabitants of the town had died by some strange death. Each and every one of them was standing motionless with two drops of blood from his mouth congealed upon his coat. When I touched one of them his head toppled and fell to the ground.

I came to a butcher's shop and saw there a man like the odds-and-ends man in front of our house. He had a scarf wrapped around his neck and held a long-bladed knife in his hand and he stared at me with red eyes from which the lids seemed to have been cut off. I tried to take the knife from his hand. His head toppled and fell to the ground. I fled in terror. As I ran along the streets everyone I saw was standing motionless. When I reached my father-in-law's house my brother-in-law, the bitch's little brother, was sitting on the stone bench outside. I put my hand into my pocket, took out a pair of cakes and tried to put them into his hand, but the moment I touched him his head toppled and fell to the ground. I shrieked aloud and awoke.

The room was still half dark. My heart was beating hard. I felt as if the ceiling were weighing down upon my head and the walls had grown immensely thick and threatened to crush me. My eyes had become dim. I lay for some time in terror, counting and re-counting the uprights of the walls. I had hardly shut my eyes when I heard a noise. It was Nanny, who had come to tidy up the room. She had laid breakfast for me in a room in the upper storey. I went upstairs and sat down by the sash window. From up there the old odds-and-ends man in front of my window was out of sight but I could see the butcher over on the left. His movements which, seen from my own window, seemed heavy, deliberate and frightening, now struck me as helpless, even comical. I felt that this man had no business to be a butcher at all and was only acting a part. A man led up the two gaunt, black horses with their deep, hollow cough. Each of them had a pair of sheep carcases slung across its back. The butcher ran his greasy hand over his moustache and appraised the carcases with a buyer's eye. Then, with an effort, he carried two of them across and hung them from the hook at the entrance to the shop. I saw him pat their legs. I have no doubt that when he stroked his wife's body at night he would think of the sheep and reflect how much he could make if he were to kill his wife.

When the tidying-up was finished I went back to my room and made a resolution, a frightful resolution. I went into the little closet off my room and took out a bone-handled knife which I kept in a box there. I wiped the blade on the skirt of my caftan and hid it under the pillow. I had made this resolution a long time before but there had been something just now in the movements of the butcher as he cut up the legs of the sheep, weighed out the meat and then looked around with an expression of self-satisfaction which somehow made me want to imitate him. This was a pleasure that I too must experience. I could see from my window a patch of perfect, deep blue in the midst of the clouds. It seemed to me that I should have to climb a very long ladder to reach that patch of sky. The horizon was covered with thick, yellow, deathly clouds which weighed heavily upon the whole city.

It was horrible, delicious weather. For some reason which I cannot explain I crouched down to the floor. In this kind of weather I always tended to think of death. But it was only now, when death, his face smeared with blood, was clutching my throat with his bony hands, that I made up my mind. I made up my mind to take the bitch with me, to prevent her from saying when I had gone, 'God have mercy on him, his troubles are over.'

A funeral procession passed by in front of my window. The coffin was draped with black and a lighted candle stood upon it. My ear caught the cry, *'La elaha ell' Allah'*.* All the tradespeople and the passersby left whatever they were doing and walked seven paces after the coffin. Even the butcher came out, walked the regulation seven paces after the coffin and returned to his shop. But the old pedlar-man did not stir from his place beside his wares. How serious everybody suddenly looked! Doubtless their thoughts had turned abruptly to the subject of death and the after-life. When my nurse brought me my medicine I observed that she looked thoughtful. She was fingering the beads of a large rosary and was muttering some formula to herself. Then she took up her position outside my door, beat her breast and recited her prayers in a loud voice: 'My God! My Go-o-o-d!'

*'There is no god but God', part of the Moslem profession of faith.

Anyone might have thought it was my business to pardon the living! All this buffoonery left me completely cold. It actually gave me a certain satisfaction to think that, for a few seconds at any rate, the rabble-men were undergoing, temporarily and superficially it is true, something of what I was suffering. Was not my room a coffin? This bed that was always unrolled, inviting me to sleep, was it not colder and darker than the grave? The thought that I was lying in a coffin had occurred to me several times. At night my room seemed to contract and to press against my body. May it not be that people have this same sensation in the grave? Is anything definite known about the sensations we may experience after death? True, the blood ceases to circulate and after the lapse of twenty-four hours certain parts of the body begin to decompose. Nevertheless the hair and the nails continue to grow for some time after death. Do sensation and thought cease as soon as the heart has stopped beating or do they continue a vague existence, alimented by the blood still remaining in the minor blood-vessels? The fact of dying is a fearful thing in itself but the consciousness that one is dead would be far worse. Some old men die with a smile on their lips like people passing from sleep into a deeper sleep or like a lamp burning out. What must be the sensations of a young, strong man who dies suddenly and who continues for some time longer to struggle against death with all the strength of his being?

I had many times reflected on the fact of death and on the decomposition of the component parts of my body, so that this idea had ceased to frighten me. On the contrary, I genuinely longed to pass into oblivion and nonbeing. The only thing I feared was that the atoms of my body should later go to make up the bodies of rabble-men. This thought was unbearable to me. There were times when I wished I could be endowed after death with large hands with long, sensitive fingers: I would carefully collect together all the atoms of my body and hold them tightly in my hands to prevent them, my property, from passing into the bodies of rabble-men.

Sometimes I imagined that the visions I saw were those which appeared to everyone who was at the point of death. All anxiety, awe, fear and will to live had subsided within me and my renunciation of the religious beliefs which had been inculcated into me in my childhood had given me an extraordinary inner tranquillity. What comforted me was the prospect of oblivion after death. The thought of an afterlife frightened and fatigued me. I had never been able to adapt myself to the world in which I was now living. Of what use would another world be to me? I felt that this world had not been made for me but for a tribe of brazen, money-grubbing, blustering louts, sellers of conscience, hungry of eye and heart—for people, in fact, who had been created in its own likeness and who fawned and grovelled before the mighty of earth and heaven as the hungry dog outside the butcher's shop wagged his tail in the hope of receiving a fragment of offal. The thought of an afterlife frightened and fatigued me. No, I had no desire to see all these loathsome worlds peopled with repulsive faces. Was God such a parvenu that He insisted on my looking over His collection of worlds? I must speak as I think. If I had to go through another life, then I hoped that my mind and senses would be numb. In that event I could exist without effort and weariness. I would live my life in the shadow of the columns of some lingam temple. I would retire into some corner where the light of the sun would never strike my eyes and the words of men and the noise of life never grate upon my ears.

I retired as deep as I could into the depths of my own being like an animal that hides itself in a cave in the wintertime. I heard other people's voices with my ears; my own I heard in my throat. The solitude that surrounded me was like the deep, dense night of eternity, that night of dense, clinging, contagious darkness which awaits the moment when it will descend upon silent cities full of dreams of lust and rancour. From the viewpoint of this throat with which I had identified myself I was nothing more than an insane abstract mathematical demonstration. The pressure which, in the act of procreation, holds together two people who are striving to escape from their solitude is the result of this same streak of madness which exists in every person, mingled with regret at the thought that he is slowly sliding towards the abyss of death. . . .

Only death does not lie.

The presence of death annihilates all superstitions. We are the children of death and it is death that rescues us from the deceptions of life. In the midst of life he calls us and summons us to him. At an age when we have not yet learnt the language of men if at times we pause in our play it is that we may listen to the voice of death. . . . Throughout our life death is beckoning to us. Has it not happened to everyone suddenly, without reason, to be plunged into thought and to remain immersed so deeply in it as to lose consciousness of time and place and the working of his own mind? At such times one has to make an effort in order to perceive and recognise again the phenomenal world in which men live. One has been listening to the voice of death.

Lying in this damp, sweaty bed, as my eyelids grew heavy and I longed to surrender myself to nonbeing and everlasting night, I felt that my lost memories and forgotten fears were all coming to life again: fear lest the feathers in my pillow should turn into dagger blades or the buttons on my coat expand to the size of millstones; fear lest the breadcrumbs that fell to the floor should shatter into fragments like pieces of glass; apprehension lest the oil in the lamp should spill during my sleep and set fire to the whole city; anxiety lest the paws of the dog outside the butcher's shop should ring like horses' hoofs as they struck the ground; dread lest the old odds-and-ends man sitting behind his wares should burst into laughter and be unable to stop; fear lest the worms in the footbath by the tank in our courtyard should turn into Indian serpents; fear lest my bedclothes should turn into a hinged gravestone above me and the marble teeth should lock, preventing me from ever escaping; panic fear lest I should suddenly lose the faculty of speech and, however much I might try to call out, nobody should ever come to my aid. . . .

I used to try to recall the days of my childhood but when I succeeded in doing so and experienced that time again it was as grim and painful as the present.

Other things which brought their contribution of anxiety and fear were my coughing, which sounded like that of the gaunt, black horses in front of the butcher's shop; my spitting, and the fear lest the phlegm should some day reveal a streak of blood, the tepid, salty liquid which rises from the depths of the body, the juice of life, which we must vomit up in the end; and the continuous menace of death, which smashes forever the fabric of the mind and passes on.

Life as it proceeds reveals, coolly and dispassionately, what lies behind the mask that each man wears. It would seem that everyone possesses several faces. Some people use only one all the time, and it then, naturally, becomes soiled and wrinkled. These are the thrifty sort. Others look after their masks in the hope of passing them on to their descendants. Others again are constantly changing their faces. But all of them, when they reach old age, realise one day that the mask they are wearing is their last and that it will soon be worn out, and then, from behind the last mask, the real face appears.

The walls of my room must have contained some virus that poisoned all my thoughts. I felt sure that before me some murderer, some diseased madman, had lived in it. Not only the walls of the room itself, but the view from the window, the butcher, the old odds-and-ends man, my nurse, the bitch and everyone whom I used to see, even the bowl from which I ate my barley broth and the clothes that I wore—all these had conspired together to engender such thoughts in my brain.

A few nights ago when I took off my clothes in a cubicle at the bathhouse my thoughts took a new direction. As the attendant poured water over my head I felt as though my black thoughts were being washed away. I observed my shadow on the steamy wall of the bathhouse. I saw that I was as frail and thin as I had been ten years earlier, when I was a child. I remembered distinctly that my shadow had fallen then in just the same way on the wet wall of the bathhouse. I looked down at my body. There was something lascivious and yet hopeless in the look of my thighs, calves and loins. Their shadow too had not changed since ten years before, when I was only a child. I felt that my whole life had passed without purpose or meaning like the flickering shadows on the bathhouse wall. Other people were massive, solid, thick-necked. Doubtless the shadows they cast on the steamy wall of the bathhouse were bigger and denser and left their imprint for some moments after they had gone, whereas mine was effaced instantaneously. When I had finished dressing after the bath my gestures and thoughts seemed to change again. It was as though I had entered a different world, as though I had been born again in the old world that I detested. At all events I could say that I had acquired a new life, for it seemed a miracle to me that I had not dissolved in the bath like a lump of salt.

My life appeared to me just as strange, as unnatural, as inexplicable, as the picture on the pen case that I am using this moment as I write. I feel that the design on the lid of this pen case must have been drawn by an artist in the grip of some mad obsession. Often when my eye lights on this picture it strikes me as somehow familiar. Perhaps this picture is the reason why . . . Perhaps it is this picture that impels me to write. It represents a cypress tree at the foot of which is squatting a bent old man like an Indian fakir. He has a long cloak wrapped about him and he is wearing a turban on his head. The index finger of his left hand is pressed to his lips in a gesture of surprise. Before him a girl in a long black dress is dancing. Her movements are not those of ordinary people—she could be Bugam Dasi. She is holding a flower of morning glory in her hand. Between them runs a little stream.

I was sitting beside my opium brazier. All my dark thoughts had dissolved and vanished in the subtle heavenly smoke. My body was meditating, my body was dreaming and gliding through space. It seemed to have been released from the burden and contamination of the lower air and to be soaring in an unknown world of strange colours and shapes. The opium had breathed its vegetable soul, its sluggish, vegetable soul, into my frame, and I lived and moved in a world of vegetable existence. But as, with my cloak over my shoulders, I drowsed beside the leather ground-sheet on which my brazier stood, the thought of the old odds-and-ends man for some reason came to my mind. He used to sit huddled up beside his wares in the same posture as I was then in. The thought struck me with horror. I rose, threw off the cloak and stood in front of the mirror. My cheeks were inflamed to the colour of the meat that hangs in front of butchers' shops. My beard was dishevelled. And yet there was something immaterial, something fascinating, in the reflection that I saw. The eyes wore an expression of weariness and suffering like those of a sick child. It was as though everything that was heavy, earthy and human in me had melted away. I was pleased with my face. I inspired in myself a certain voluptuous satisfaction. As I looked into the mirror I said to myself, 'Your pain is so profound that it has settled in the depths of your eyes . . . and, if you weep, the tears will come from the very depths of your eyes or they will not come at all.' Then I said, 'You are a fool. Why don't you put an end to yourself here and now? What are you waiting for? What have you to hope for now? Have you forgotten the bottle of wine in the closet? One gulp, and there's an end of everything. . . . Fool! . . . You are a fool! . . . Here I am, talking to the air!'

The thoughts which came into my mind were unrelated to one another. I could hear my voice in my throat but I could not grasp the meaning of the words. The sounds were mingled in my brain with other sounds. My fingers seemed bigger than normal, as always when the fever was on me. My eyelids felt heavy, my lips had grown thick. I turned round and saw my nurse standing in the doorway. I burst out laughing. My nurse's face was motionless. Her lusterless eyes were fixed on me but they were empty of surprise, irritation or sadness. Generally speaking, it is ordinary stupid conduct that makes one laugh, but this laughter of mine arose from a deeper cause. The vast stupidity that I saw before me was part of the general inability of mankind to unravel the central problems of existence and that thing which for her was shrouded in impenetrable darkness was a gesture of death itself.

She took the brazier and walked with deliberation out of the room. I wiped the sweat from my forehead. My hands were covered with white flecks. I leaned against the wall, pressing my head to the bricks, and began to feel better. After a little I murmured the words of a song which I had heard somewhere or other:

> *'Come, let us go and drink wine;*
> *Let us drink wine of the Kingdom of Rey.*
> *If we do not drink now, when should we drink?'*

When the crisis was coming upon me I could always feel its approach in advance and was filled with an extraordinary uneasiness and depression as though a cord had been tied tightly around my heart. My mood was like the weather before the storm breaks. At such times the real world receded from me and I lived in a radiant world incalculably remote from that of earth.

Then I was afraid of myself and of everyone else. I suppose this condition of mine was due to my illness, which had sapped my mental strength. The sight of the old odds-and-ends man and the butcher through the window filled me with fear. There was something frightening in their gestures and in their faces. My nurse told me a frightful thing. She swore by all the prophets that she had seen the old odds-and-ends man come to my wife's room during the night and that from behind the door she had heard the bitch say to him, 'Take your scarf off.' It does not bear thinking of. Two or three days ago when I shrieked out and my wife came and stood in the doorway, I saw, I saw with my own eyes, that her lips bore the imprint of the old man's dirty yellow, decayed teeth, between which he used to recite the Arabic verses of the Koran. And, now I came to think of it, why was it that this man had been hanging about outside our house ever since I had got married? Was he one of the bitch's lovers? I remember I went over that same day to where the old man was sitting beside his wares and asked him how much he wanted for his jar. He looked at me over the folds of the scarf that muffled his face. Two decayed teeth emerged from under the harelip and he burst into laughter. It was a grating, hollow laugh, of a quality to make the hairs on one's body stand on end. He said, 'Do you usually buy things without looking at them? This jar's not worth bothering about. Take it, young man. Hope it brings you luck.' His voice had a peculiar tone as he said, 'Not worth bothering about. Hope it brings you luck.' I put my hand into my pocket and took out two *dirhems** and four *peshiz** which I laid on the corner of the canvas sheet. He burst into laughter again. It was a grating laugh, of a quality to make the hairs on one's body stand on end. I could have sunk into the ground with shame. I covered my face with my hands and walked back to the house.

*Mediaeval coins, corresponding roughly to the modern *kran* and *abbasi* respectively.

From all the articles laid out before him came a rusty smell as of dirty discarded objects which life had rejected. Perhaps his aim was to show people the discarded things of life and to draw attention to them. After all, was he not old and discarded himself? All the articles in his collection were dead, dirty and unserviceable. But what a stubborn life was in them and what significance there was in their forms! These dead objects left a far deeper imprint upon my mind than living people could ever have done.

But Nanny had told me this story about him and had passed it on to everyone else. . . . With a dirty beggar! My nurse told me that my wife's bed had become infested with lice and she had gone to the baths. I wonder how her shadow looked on the steamy wall of the bathhouse. No doubt it was a voluptuous shadow with plenty of self-confidence. All things considered, my wife's taste in men did not offend me this time. The old odds-and-ends man was not a commonplace, flat, insipid creature like the stud-males that stupid randy women usually fall for. The old man with his ailments, with the rind of misfortune that encrusted him and the misery that emanated from him, was, probably without realising it himself, a kind of small-scale exhibition organised by God for the edification of mankind. As he sat there with his squalid collection of wares on the ground in front of him, he was a sample and a personification of the whole creation.

Yes, I had seen on my wife's face the mark of the two dirty, decayed teeth between which he used to recite the Arabic verses of the Koran. This was the same wife who would not let me come near her, who scorned me, and whom I loved in spite of everything, in spite of the fact that she had never once allowed me to kiss her on the lips.

The sun was setting. From somewhere came the high-pitched, plaintive sound of a kettledrum. It was a sound expressive of entreaty and supplication, which awoke in me all my ancestral superstitions and, with them, my fear of the dark. The crisis, the approach of which I had felt in advance and which I was expecting from moment to moment, came upon me. My whole body was filled with burning heat and I felt that I was suffocating. I collapsed onto my bed and shut my eyes. It seemed to me in my feverish condition that everything had expanded and had lost all distinctness of outline. The ceiling, instead of sinking, had risen. I felt oppressed by the weight of my clothes. For no reason I stood up and sat down again upon my bed, murmuring to myself, 'The thing has reached the limit . . . This is beyond endurance. . . .' Then I stopped abruptly. After a little I began again slowly and distinctly, in an ironical tone of voice: 'The thing has . . .' I stopped, and added, 'I am a fool'. I paid no attention to the meaning of the words I uttered. I was merely amusing myself with the vibration of my voice in the air. Perhaps I was talking to my shadow in order to dispel my loneliness.

And then I saw an incredible thing. The door opened and the bitch came into the room. So then, she used to think of me at times and in spite of everything I still had reason to feel grateful to her. She knew that I was still alive, that I was suffering, that I was slowly dying. In spite of everything I still had reason to feel grateful to her. I only wondered whether she knew that I was dying because of her. If she did know that I would die perfectly happy. At that moment I was the happiest man on the face of the earth. Merely by coming into the room the bitch had driven away all my evil thoughts. Some sort of radiation emanated from her, from her movements, and brought me relief. On this occasion she was in better health than when I had last seen her. She was plump and comfortable-looking. She had on a cloak of Tus material. Her eyebrows were plucked and were stained with indigo. She was wearing a beauty spot and her face was made up with rouge, ceruse and kohl. In a word she was turned out to perfection. She appeared to be well pleased with life. She was unconsciously holding the index finger of her left hand to her lips. Was this the same graceful creature, was this the slim, ethereal girl who, in a black pleated dress, had played hide-and-seek with me on the bank of the Suran, the unconstrained, childlike, frail girl whose ankles, appearing from under her skirt, had so excited me? Until this moment, when I had looked at her I had not seen her as she really was. Now it was as though a veil had fallen from my eyes. For some reason the thought of the sheep hanging by the door of the butcher's shop occurred to me. She had become for me the equivalent of a lump of butcher's meat. Her old enchantment had gone. She had become a comfortable, solid woman with a head full of commonplace, practical ideas—a genuine woman. I realised with affright that my wife was now a grown-up while I had remained a child. I actually felt ashamed in her presence, under her gaze. This woman who yielded her body to everyone but me while I consoled myself with fanciful memories of her childhood, when her face was simple and innocent and wore a dreamy, fleeting expression, this woman whose face still bore the tooth-marks of the old odds-and-ends man in the square—no, this was not the same person as I had known.

She asked me in a sarcastic tone, 'How are you feeling?' I replied, 'Aren't you perfectly free? Don't you do everything you feel like doing? What does my health matter to you?'

She left the room, slamming the door behind her. She did not turn to look at me. It seems as though I have forgotten how to talk to the people of this world, to living people. She, the woman who I had thought was devoid of all feelings, was offended at my behaviour! Several times I thought of getting up and going to her to fall at her feet, weeping and asking her to forgive me. Yes, weeping; for I thought that if only I could weep I should find relief. Some time passed; whether it was to be measured in minutes, hours or centuries I do not know. I had become like a madman and I derived an exquisite pleasure from the pain I felt. It was a pleasure which transcended human experience, a pleasure which only I was capable of feeling and which the gods themselves, if they existed, could not have experienced to such a degree. At that moment I was conscious of my superiority. I felt my superiority to the men of the rabble, to nature and to the gods—the gods, that product of human lusts. I had become a god. I was greater than God, and I felt within me the eternal, infinite flux. . . .

She came back. So then she was not as cruel as I had thought. I rose, kissed the hem of her dress and fell at her feet, weeping and coughing. I rubbed my face against her leg and several times I called her by her real name. It seemed to me that the sound of her real name had a peculiar ring. And at the same time in my heart, in the bottom of my heart, I said, 'Bitch . . . bitch!' I kissed her legs; the skin tasted like the stub end of a cucumber, faintly acrid and bitter. I wept and wept. How much time passed so I do not know. When I came to myself she had gone. It may be that the space of time in which I had experienced all the pleasures, the caresses and the pain of which the nature of man is susceptible had not lasted more than a moment. I was alone, in the same posture as when I used to sit with my opium pipe beside the brazier, sitting by my smoky oil lamp like the old odds-and-ends man behind his wares. I did not budge from my place but sat watching the smoke of the lamp. Particles of soot from the flame settled on my hands and face like black snow. My nurse came in with my supper, a bowl of barley broth and a plate of greasy chicken pilaff. She uttered a scream of terror, dropped the tray and ran out of the room. It pleased me to think that I was able at any rate to frighten her. I rose to my feet, snuffed the lamp wick and stood in front of the mirror. I smeared the particles of soot over my face. How frightful was the face that I saw! I pulled down my lower eyelids, released them, tugged at the corners of my mouth, puffed out my cheeks, pulled the tip of my beard upwards and twisted it out to the sides and grimaced at myself. My face had a natural talent for comical and horrible expressions. I felt that they enabled me to see with my own eyes all the weird shapes, all the comical, horrible, unbelievable images which lurked in the recesses of my mind. They were all familiar to me, I felt them within me, and yet at the same time they struck me as comical. All of these grimacing faces existed inside me and formed part of me: horrible, criminal, ludicrous masks which changed at a single movement of my fingertip. The old Koran-reader, the butcher, my wife—I saw all of them within me. They were reflected in me as in a mirror; the forms of all of them existed inside me but none of them belonged to me. Were not the substance and the expressions of my face the result of a mysterious sequence of impulsions, of my ancestors' temptations, lusts and despairs? And I who was the custodian of the heritage, did I not, through some mad, ludicrous feeling, consider it my duty, whether I liked it or not, to preserve this stock of facial expressions?

Probably my face would be released from this responsibility and would assume its own natural expression only at the moment of my death. . . . But even then would not the expressions which had been incised on my face by a sardonic resolve leave their traces behind, too deeply engraved to be effaced? At all events I now knew what possibilities existed within me, I appreciated my own capabilities.

Suddenly I burst into laughter. It was a harsh, grating, horrible laugh which made the hairs on my body stand on end. For I did not recognise my own laughter. It seemed to come from someone other than me. I felt that it had often reverberated in the depths of my throat and that I had heard it in the depths of my ears. Simultaneously I began to cough. A clot of bloody phlegm, a fragment of my inside, fell onto the mirror. I wiped it across the glass with my fingertip. I turned round and saw Nanny staring at me. She was horror-stricken. She was holding in her hand a bowl of barley broth which she had brought me, thinking that I might now be able to eat my supper. I covered my face with my hands and ran behind the curtain which hung across the entrance to the closet.

Later, as I was falling asleep, I felt as though my head was clamped in a fiery ring. The sharp exciting perfume of sandalwood oil with which I had filled my lamp penetrated my nostrils. It contained within it the odour of my wife's legs, and I felt in my mouth the faintly bitter taste of the stub end of a cucumber. I ran my hand over my body and mentally compared it—thighs, calves, arms and the rest—with my wife's. I could see again the line of her thigh and buttocks, could feel the warmth of her body. The illusion was far stronger than a mere mental picture; it had the force of a physical need. I wanted to feel her body close to mine. A single gesture, a single effort of the will would have been enough to dispel the voluptuous temptation. Then the fiery ring around my head grew so tight and so burning hot that I sank deep into a mysterious sea peopled with terrifying shapes.

It was still dark when I was awakened by the voices of a band of drunken policemen who were marching along the street, joking obscenely among themselves. Then they sang in chorus,

'Come, let us go and dririk wine;
Let us drink wine of the Kingdom of Rey.
If we do not drink now, when should we drink?'

I remembered—no, I had a sudden flash of inspiration: I had some wine in the closet, a bottle of wine which contained a portion of cobra venom. One gulp of that wine and all the nightmares of life would fade as though they had never been. . . . But what about the bitch? . . . The word intensified my longing for her, brought her before me full of vitality and warmth. What better could I do than give her a glass of that wine and drink off another myself? Then we should die together in a single convulsion. What is love? For the rabble-men it is an obscenity, a carnal, ephemeral thing. The rabble-men must needs express their love in lascivious songs, in obscenities and in the foul phrases they are always repeating, drunk or sober—'shoving the donkey's hoof into the mud', 'giving the ground a thump', and so forth. Love for her meant something different to me. True, I had known her for many years. Her strange, slanting eyes, small, half-open mouth, husky, soft voice—all of these things were charged with distant, painful memories and in all of them I sought something of which I had been deprived, something that was intimately connected with my being and which had been taken from me.

Had I been deprived of this thing for all time to come? The fear that it might be so aroused in me a grimmer feeling. The thought of the other pleasure, the one which might compensate me for my hopeless love, had become a kind of obsession. For some reason the figure of the butcher opposite the window of my room occurred to me. I remembered how he would roll up his sleeves, utter the sacred formula *'besmellah'** and proceed to cut up his meat. His expression and attitude were always present to my mind. In the end

*'In the name of God.' The formula pronounced by Moslems at the beginning of any important undertaking.

I too came to a decision, a frightful decision. I got out of bed, rolled up my sleeves and took out the bone-handled knife which I had hidden underneath my pillow. I stooped and threw a yellow cloak over my shoulders and muffled my neck and face in a scarf. I felt that as I did so I assumed an attitude of mind which was a cross between that of the butcher and that of the old odds-and-ends man.

Then I went on tip-toe towards my wife's room. When I reached it I found that it was quite dark. I softly opened the door. She seemed to be dreaming. She cried, loudly and distinctly, 'Take your scarf off.' I went over to her bedside and bent down until I could feel her warm, even breath upon my face. What pleasant warmth and vitality there was in her breath! It seemed to me that if only I could breathe in this warmth for a while I should come to life again. I had thought for so long that other people's breath must be burning hot like mine. I looked around carefully to see if there was anyone else in the room, to make sure that none of her lovers was there. She was alone. I realised that all the things people said about her were mere slander. How did I know that she was not still a virgin? I was ashamed of all my unfair suspicions.

This sensation lasted only a minute. Suddenly from outside the door came the sound of a sneeze and I heard a stifled mocking laugh, of a quality to make the hairs on one's body stand on end. The sound contracted every nerve in my body. If I had not heard the sneeze and the laugh, if the man, whoever he was, had not given me pause,* I should have carried out my decision and cut her body into pieces. I should have given the meat to the butcher opposite our house to sell to his customers, and, in fulfilment of a special resolution, I myself should have given a piece of the flesh of her thigh to the old Koran-reader and gone to him on the following day and said, 'Do you know where that meat you ate last night came from?' If he had not laughed, I should have done this. I should have had to do it in the dark, so that I should not have been compelled to meet the bitch's eye. Her expression of reproach would have been too much for me. Finally I snatched up a piece of cloth which was trailing from her bed and in which my foot had caught and fled from the room. I tossed the knife up onto the roof, because it was the knife that had suggested the idea of murder to me. I got rid of a knife which was identical with the one I had seen in the butcher's hand.

When I got back to my room, I saw by the light of my oil lamp that the cloth I had taken with me was her nightdress: a soiled nightdress which had been in contact with her flesh; a soft, silk nightdress of Indian make. It smelt of her body and of champac perfume, and it still held something of the warmth of her body, something of her. I held

*A Persian superstition requires that, if anyone present should sneeze, any action which one may have been about to undertake be postponed.

it against my face and breathed deeply. Then I lay down, placed it between my legs and fell asleep. I had never slept as soundly as I did that night. Early in the morning I was awoken by my wife's clamours. She was lamenting the disappearance of her nightdress and kept repeating at the top of her voice, 'A brand-new nightdress!', despite the fact that it had a tear in the sleeve. I would not have given it back to her to save my life. Surely I was entitled to keep an old nightdress of my own wife's.

When Nanny brought me my ass's milk, honey and bread I found that she had placed a bone-handled knife on the tray beside the breakfast things. She said she had noticed it among the old odds-and-ends man's wares and had bought it from him. Then she said, raising her eyebrows, 'Let's hope it'll come in handy some day.' I picked it up and examined it. It was my own knife. Then Nanny said in a querulous, offended tone, 'Oh yes, my daughter' (she meant the bitch) 'was saying this morning that I stole her nightdress during the night. I don't want to have to answer for anything connected with you two. Anyway, she began to bleed yesterday. . . . I knew it was the baby. . . . According to her, she got pregnant at the baths.* I went to her room to massage her belly during

*It was popularly believed that women could become pregnant through using the public baths, which were frequented (at different hours) by men also. The belief could be exploited to provide an explanation of otherwise inexplicable pregnancies.

the night and I noticed her arms were all black and blue. She showed them to me and said, "I went down to the cellar at an unlucky time, and the Good People gave me an awful pinching."' She went on, 'Did you know your wife's been pregnant for a long time?' I laughed and said, 'I dare say the child'll look like the old man that reads the Koran. I suppose it gave its first leap when she was looking at the old man's face.'* Nanny looked at me indignantly and went out of the room. Apparently she had not expected such a reply. I rose hastily, picked up the bone-handled knife with a trembling hand, put it away in the box in the closet and shut the lid.

No, it was out of the question that the baby should have leapt when she was looking at my face. It must have been the old odds-and-ends man.

Some time during the afternoon the door of my room opened and her little brother, the bitch's little brother, came in, biting his nail. You could tell the moment you saw them that they were brother and sister. The resemblance was extraordinary. He had full, moist, sensual lips, languid, heavy eyelids, slanting, wondering eyes, high cheekbones, unruly, date-coloured hair and a complexion the colour of ripe wheat. He was the image of the bitch and he had

*Another popular belief was that a baby would resemble the person at whom the mother happened to be looking when it stirred for the first time in the womb.

a touch of her satanic spirit. His was one of those impassive, soulless Turkoman faces which are so appropriate to a people engaged in an unremitting battle with life, a people which regards any action as permissible if it helps it to go on living. Nature had shaped this brother and sister over many generations. Their ancestors had lived exposed to sun and rain, battling unceasingly with their environment, and had not only transmitted to them faces and characters modified correspondingly but had bequeathed to them a share of their stubbornness, sensuality, rapacity and hungriness. I remembered the taste of his lips, faintly bitter, like that of the stub end of a cucumber.

When he came into the room he looked at me with his wondering Turkoman eyes and said, 'Mummy says the doctor said you are going to die and it'll be a good riddance for us. How do people die?'

I said, 'Tell her I have been dead for a long time.'

'Mummy said, "If I hadn't had a miscarriage the whole house would have belonged to us."'

I involuntarily burst out laughing. It was a hollow, grating laugh, of a quality to make the hairs on one's body stand on end. I did not recognise the sound of my own voice. The child ran from the room in terror.

I realised then why it was that the butcher found it pleasant to wipe the blade of his bone-handled knife on the legs of the sheep. The pleasure of cutting up the raw meat in which the dead, coagulated blood had settled, like slime on the bottom of a tank, while a watery liquid dripped from the windpipes onto the ground—the yellow dog outside the shop, the severed oxhead on the floor, staring dimly, and the heads of the sheep themselves with the dust of death on their eyes, they too had seen this, they too knew what the butcher felt.

I understood now that I had become a miniature God. I had transcended the mean, paltry needs of mankind and felt within me the flux of eternity. What is eternity? To me eternity meant to play hide-and-seek with the bitch on the bank of the Suran, to shut my eyes for a single moment and hide my face in the skirt of her dress.

All at once I realised that I was talking to myself and that in a strange way. I was trying to talk to myself but my lips had become so heavy that they were incapable of the least movement. Yet although my lips did not stir and I could not hear my voice I felt that I was talking to myself.

In this room which was steadily shrinking and growing dark like the grave, night had surrounded me with its fearful shadows. In the light of the smoky oil lamp my shadow, in the sheepskin jacket, cloak and scarf that I was wearing, was stretched motionless across the wall. The shadow that I cast upon the wall was much denser and more distinct than my real body. My shadow had become more real than myself. The old odds-and-ends man, the butcher, Nanny and the bitch, my wife, were shadows of me, shadows in the midst of which I was imprisoned. I had become like a screech owl, but my cries caught in my throat and I spat them out in the form of clots of blood. Perhaps screech owls are subject to a disease which makes them think as I think. My shadow on the wall had become exactly like an owl and, leaning forward, read intently every word I wrote. Without doubt he understood perfectly. Only he was capable of understanding. When I looked out of the corner of my eye at my shadow on the wall I felt afraid.

It was a dark, silent night like the night which had enveloped all my being, a night peopled with fearful shapes which grimaced at me from door and wall and curtain. At times my room became so narrow that I felt that I was lying in a coffin. My temples were burning. My limbs were incapable of the least movement. A weight was pressing on my chest like the weight of the carcases they sling over the backs of horses and deliver to the butchers.

Death was murmuring his song in my ear like a stammering man who is obliged to repeat each word and who, when he has come to the end of a line, has to begin it afresh. His song penetrated my flesh like the whine of a saw. He would raise his voice and suddenly fall silent.

My eyes were not yet closed when a band of drunken policemen marched by in the street outside my room, joking obscenely among themselves. Then they sang in chorus,

'Come, let us go and drink wine;
Let us drink wine of the Kingdom of Rey.
If we do not drink now, when should we drink?'

I said to myself, 'Since the police are going to get me in the end . . .' Suddenly I felt within me a superhuman force. My forehead grew cool. I rose, threw a yellow cloak over my shoulders and wrapped my scarf two or three times around my neck. I bent down, went into the closet and took out the bone-handled knife which I had hidden in the box. Then I went on tip-toe towards the bitch's room. When I reached the door I saw that the room was in complete darkness. I listened and heard her voice saying, 'Have you come? Take your scarf off.' Her voice had a pleasant quality, as it had had in her childhood. It reminded me of the unconscious murmuring of someone who is dreaming. I myself had heard this voice in the past when I was in a deep sleep. Was she dreaming? Her voice was husky and thick. It had become like the voice of the little girl who had played hide-and-seek with me on the bank of the Suran. I stood motionless. Then I heard her say again. 'Come in. Take your scarf off.'

I walked softly into the dark room. I took off my cloak and scarf and the rest of my clothes and crept into her bed. For some reason I kept the bone-handled knife in my hand. It seemed to me that the warmth of her bed infused a new life into me. I remembered the pale, thin little girl with the big, strange Turkoman eyes with whom I had played hide-and-seek on the bank of the Suran, and I clasped her pleasant, moist, warm body in my arms. Clasped her? No, I sprang upon her like a savage, hungry beast and in the bottom of my heart I loathed her. To me love and hatred were twins. Her fresh, moonlight-pale body, my wife's body, opened and enclosed me within itself like a cobra coiling around its prey. The perfume of her bosom made my head swim, the flesh of the arm which encircled my neck was soft and warm. I wished that my life could cease at that moment, for the hatred, the rancour that I felt for her had vanished and I tried to hold back my tears.

Her legs somehow locked behind mine like those of a mandrake and her arms held me firmly by the neck. I felt the pleasant warmth of that young flesh. Every atom in my burning body drank in that warmth. I felt that I was her prey and she was drawing me into herself. I was filled with mingled terror and delight. Her mouth was bitter to the taste, like the stub end of a cucumber. Under the pleasant pressure of her embrace, I streamed with sweat. I was beside myself with passion.

I was dominated by my body, by each atom of my material being, and they shouted aloud their song of victory. Doomed, helpless in this boundless sea, I bowed my head in surrender before the stormy passion of the waves. Her hair, redolent of champac, clung about my face, and a cry of anguish and joy burst forth from the depths of our beings. Suddenly I felt that she was biting my lip savagely, so savagely that she bit it through. Used she to bite her nail in this way or had she realised that I was not the hare lipped old man? I tried to break free from her but was unable to make the slightest movement. My efforts were useless. The flesh of our bodies had been soldered into one.

I thought to myself that she had gone mad. As we struggled, I involuntarily jerked my hand. I felt the knife, which I was still holding, sink somewhere into her flesh. A warm liquid spurted into my face. She uttered a shriek and released me. Keeping my fist clenched on the warm liquid in my hand, I tossed the knife away. I ran my other hand over her body. It was utterly cold. She was dead. And then I burst into a fit of coughing—but no, it was not coughing, it was a hollow grating laugh, of a quality to make the hairs on one's body stand on end. In terror I threw my cloak over my shoulders and hurried back to my own room. I opened my hand in the light of the oil lamp: in the palm of my hand lay her eye, and I was drenched in blood.

I went over and stood before the mirror. Overcome with horror, I covered my face with my hands. What I had seen in the mirror was the likeness, no, the exact image, of the old odds-and-ends man. My hair and beard were completely white, like those of a man who has come out alive from a room in which he has been shut up along with a cobra. My eyes were without lashes, a clump of white hairs sprouted from my chest and a new spirit had taken possession of my body. My mind and my senses were operating in a completely different way from before. A demon had awoken to life within me and I was unable to escape from him. Still holding my hands before my face, I involuntarily burst into laughter. It was a more violent laugh than the previous one had been and it made me shudder from head to foot. It was a laugh so deep that it was impossible to guess from what remote recess of the body it proceeded, a hollow laugh which came from somewhere deep down in my body and merely echoed in my throat. I had become the old odds-and-ends man.

5

THE VIOLENCE OF MY AGITATION SEEMED TO HAVE awakened me from a long, deep sleep. I rubbed my eyes. I was back in my own room. It was half-dark and outside a wet mist pressed against the windowpanes. Somewhere in the distance a cock crowed. The charcoal in the brazier beside me had burnt to cold ashes which I could have blown away with a single breath. I felt that my mind had become hollow and ashy like the coals and was at the mercy of a single breath.

The first thing I looked for was the flower vase of Rhages which the old hearse-driver had given me in the cemetery, but it had gone. I looked around and saw beside the door someone with a crouching shadow—no, it was a bent old man with his face partly concealed by a scarf wrapped around his neck. He was holding under his arm something resembling a jar, wrapped in a dirty handkerchief. He burst into a hollow, grating laugh, of a quality to make the hairs on one's body stand on end.

The moment that I made a move, he slipped out through the doorway. I got up quickly, intending to run after him and get the jar, or whatever it was that was wrapped in the handkerchief, from him, but he was already a good way off. I went back to my room and opened the window. Down the street I could still see the old man's crouching figure. His shoulders were shaking with laughter and he held the bundle tucked under his arm. He was running with all his might and in the end he disappeared into the mist. I turned away from the window and looked down at myself. My clothes were torn and soiled from top to bottom with congealed blood. Two blister-flies were circling about me, and tiny white maggots were wriggling on my coat. And on my chest I felt the weight of a woman's dead body. . . .